FUN B.C. FACTS FOR KIDS

FUN B.C. FACTS FOR KIDS

Mark Zuehlke

Whitecap Books
Vancouver / Toronto

Whitecap Books
Vancouver/Toronto

The information in this book is true and complete to the best of our knowledge. All recommendations are made without guarantee on the part of the author or Whitecap Books Ltd. The author and publisher disclaim any liability in connection with the use of this information. For additional information please contact Whitecap Books Ltd., 351 Lynn Avenue, North Vancouver, BC V7J 2C4.

Edited by Elizabeth McLean
Proofread by Peggy Trendell-Whittaker
Book design and illustration by Rose Cowles

Printed and bound in Canada.

Canadian Cataloguing in Publication Data

Zuehlke, Mark.
Fun B.C. facts for kids

Includes index.
ISBN 1-55110-404-0

1. British Columbia—Miscellanea—Juvenile literature. I. Title.
FC3811.2.Z83 1996 j971.1 C95-911141-7
F1087.4.Z83 1996

The publisher acknowledges the assistance of the Canada Council and the Cultural Services Branch of the Government of British Columbia in making this publication possible.

Acknowledgements

The information contained in this book draws heavily upon the vast wealth of information I gathered to write *The B.C. Fact Book: Everything You Ever Wanted to Know About British Columbia.* That information, and much new material tracked down exclusively for use in this book, was provided by dozens of people in federal departments, government ministries, Tourist Infocentres throughout the province, National Park and Provincial Park staff, and many others. Staff at the B.C. Archives and Records Service, the Royal British Columbia Museum, and the Vancouver Public Library contributed much useful information.

Special thanks to Sean Sharpe and Knut Atkinson for providing wildlife photos.

Diane Swanson helped me understand, and hopefully succeed at, the complex task of writing for a younger audience of readers than I had previously addressed.

Fran Backhouse was unwaveringly supportive in both word and deed. She patiently read the manuscript as it developed and provided many suggestions that, among other things, kept me walking a scientifically accurate line. Many thanks.

Contents

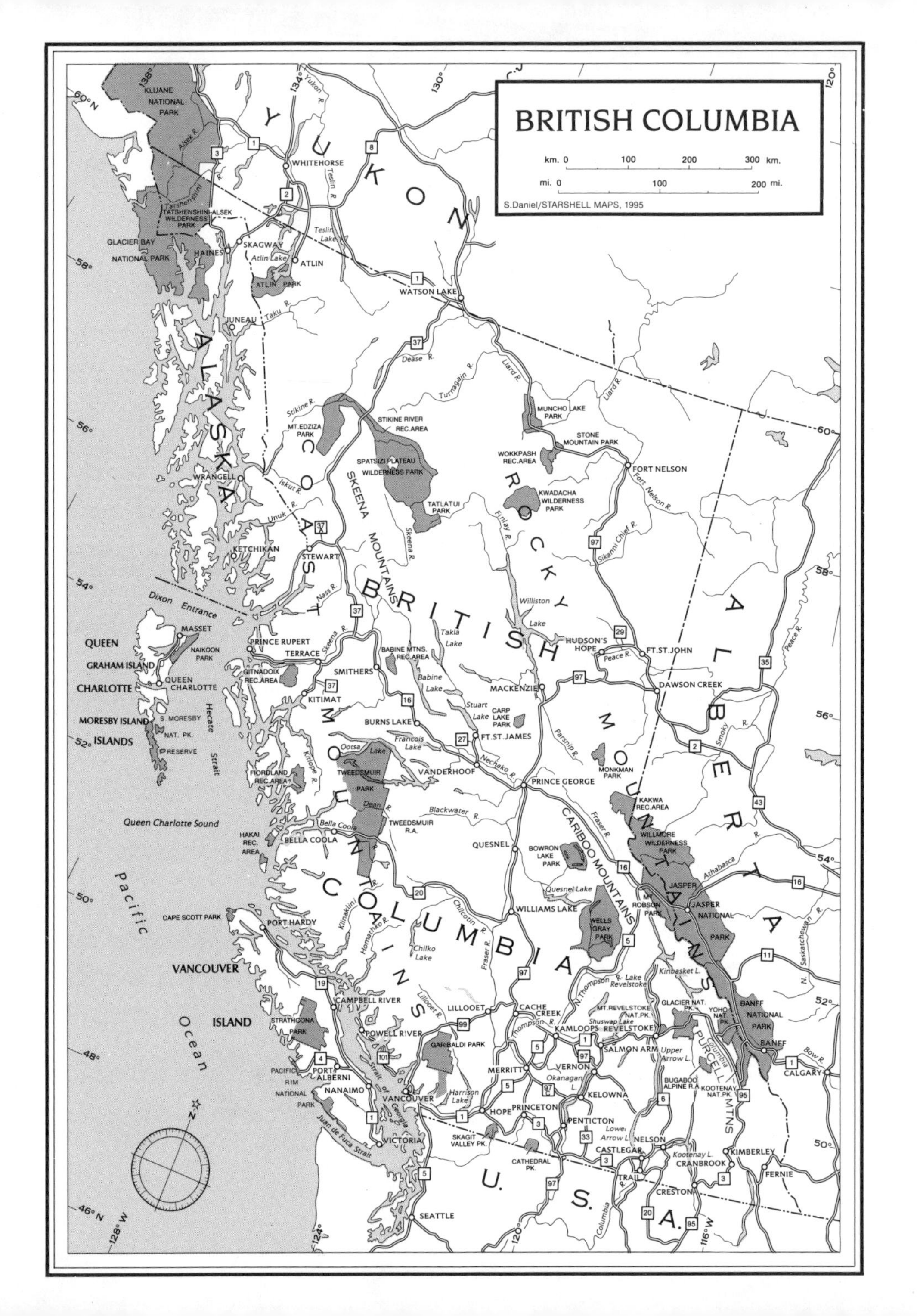
BRITISH COLUMBIA
km. 0 100 200 300 km.
mi. 0 100 200 mi.
S.Daniel/STARSHELL MAPS, 1995
YUKON
ALASKA
ALBERTA
U.S.A.
COAST MOUNTAINS
ROCKY MOUNTAINS
SKEENA MOUNTAINS
CARIBOO MOUNTAINS
PURCELL MTNS
BRITISH COLUMBIA
Pacific Ocean
QUEEN CHARLOTTE ISLANDS
GRAHAM ISLAND
MORESBY ISLAND
VANCOUVER ISLAND
Queen Charlotte Sound
Hecate Strait
Dixon Entrance
KLUANE NATIONAL PARK
TATSHENSHINI-ALSEK WILDERNESS PARK
GLACIER BAY NATIONAL PARK
WHITEHORSE
SKAGWAY
HAINES
ATLIN
ATLIN PARK
JUNEAU
WATSON LAKE
MUNCHO LAKE PARK
STONE MOUNTAIN PARK
FORT NELSON
WRANGELL
KETCHIKAN
STEWART
PRINCE RUPERT
TERRACE
SMITHERS
KITIMAT
BURNS LAKE
MASSET
QUEEN CHARLOTTE
VANDERHOOF
PRINCE GEORGE
FT.ST.JAMES
MACKENZIE
HUDSON'S HOPE
FT.ST.JOHN
DAWSON CREEK
QUESNEL
WILLIAMS LAKE
BELLA COOLA
PORT HARDY
CAMPBELL RIVER
POWELL RIVER
LILLOOET
CACHE CREEK
KAMLOOPS
REVELSTOKE
SALMON ARM
VERNON
KELOWNA
MERRITT
PENTICTON
PRINCETON
HOPE
VANCOUVER
NANAIMO
PORT ALBERNI
VICTORIA
SEATTLE
NELSON
CASTLEGAR
TRAIL
CRANBROOK
KIMBERLEY
FERNIE
CRESTON
JASPER
BANFF
CALGARY
TWEEDSMUIR PARK
WELLS GRAY PARK
GARIBALDI PARK
STRATHCONA PARK
PACIFIC RIM NATIONAL PARK
JASPER NATIONAL PARK
BANFF NATIONAL PARK
GLACIER NAT. PK.
YOHO NAT. PK.
KOOTENAY NAT. PK.
MT. REVELSTOKE NAT. PK.
MT. ROBSON PARK
WILLMORE WILDERNESS PARK
KAKWA REC. AREA
MONKMAN PARK
BOWRON LAKE PARK
SPATSIZI PLATEAU WILDERNESS PARK
STIKINE RIVER REC. AREA
MT. EDZIZA PARK
TATLATUI PARK
KWADACHA WILDERNESS PARK
WOKKPASH REC. AREA
NAIKOON PARK
S. MORESBY NAT. PK. RESERVE
CAPE SCOTT PARK
SKAGIT VALLEY PK.
CATHEDRAL PK.
Williston Lake
Fraser R.
Peace R.
Columbia R.

THE WHERE AND WHAT OF B.C.

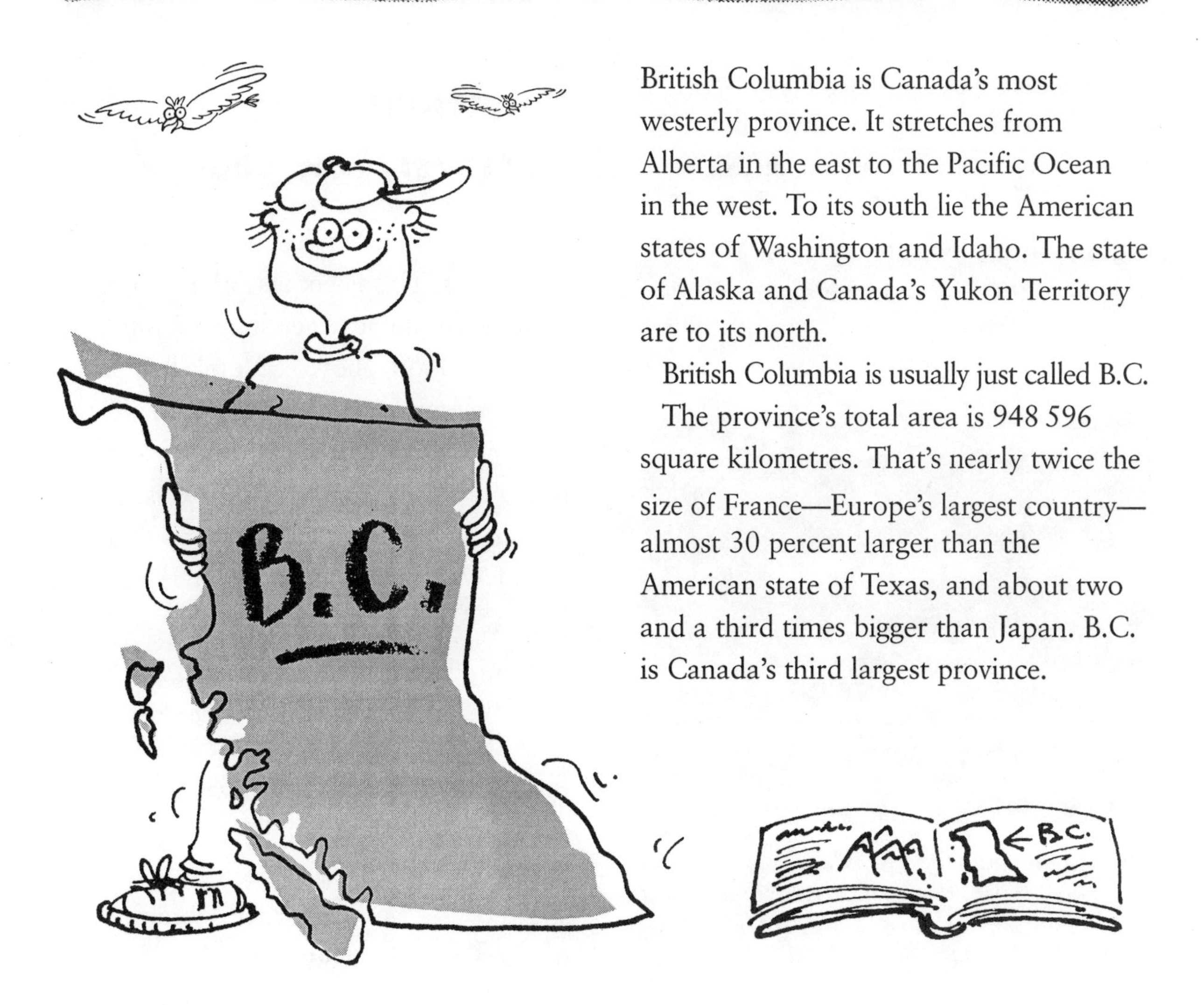

British Columbia is Canada's most westerly province. It stretches from Alberta in the east to the Pacific Ocean in the west. To its south lie the American states of Washington and Idaho. The state of Alaska and Canada's Yukon Territory are to its north.

British Columbia is usually just called B.C.

The province's total area is 948 596 square kilometres. That's nearly twice the size of France—Europe's largest country—almost 30 percent larger than the American state of Texas, and about two and a third times bigger than Japan. B.C. is Canada's third largest province.

B.C.'S GREAT COUNTRY SHOW

Glacier-cloaked mountain ranges. Sea-battered ocean shorelines. Vast rolling grasslands. Deeply shadowed ancient rainforests. Sun-soaked desert. Narrow valleys washed by tranquil lakes. You'll find all of this and more here.

The granite peak of Hound's Tooth Spire in Bugaboo Glacier Provincial Park has been carved by 70 million years of erosion by ice, wind, and rain. (BCARS photo I-08392)

Mountains Wherever You Look

Wherever you go in B.C. you will see mountains. This is because about three-quarters of the province stands 3000 metres or more above sea level. B.C. has five mountain systems. Four of these lie like thick strands of rope over the length of the province. The fifth—the Cascade Mountains—pushes like a stubby thumb out of Washington State into the southern part of B.C.

B.C.'s most easterly mountain system is the Rocky Mountains. This system is usually called the Rockies. It follows the B.C.-Alberta border northward to a little south of Fort St. John. Then it runs slightly west to a point 45 kilometres south of the Yukon border. Here the mountains fade away into a level plain.

Moving west from the Rockies, the next system is the Columbia Mountains. Running between the Rockies and the Columbia Mountains is North America's longest valley—the Rocky Mountain Trench. This remarkably narrow valley is 1400 kilometres long. But it is never more than 20 kilometres wide. The mountains form steep walls on either side of the trench.

To the west of the Columbia Mountains is the huge Interior Plateau. Unlike most plateaus, which are usually level areas of land bordered by mountains, the Interior Plateau is broken up by rolling highlands and deep, narrow valleys. The Okanagan Valley, for example, is part of the Interior Plateau. Yet the valley has little level ground and is completely surrounded by rugged mountains.

The Interior Plateau is bordered on the west by the Coast Mountains. These mountains stretch in an unbroken chain the entire length of the B.C. mainland coast.

Out to sea from the B.C. mainland are the Insular Mountains. You can't see many of these huge mountains because they are almost all under water. Only the highest parts of this range rise up out of the Pacific Ocean. The mountains and hills of Vancouver Island and the Queen Charlotte Islands are parts of the Insular Mountains you can see.

Mount Golden Hinde is Vancouver Island's highest mountain and is 2682 metres high.
(BC Parks photo 630001.1.1.15.vi)

A Snaking Coastline

In many parts of the world coastlines are quite straight. But not in British Columbia.

The coastline here twists and turns down the length of the province. It is riddled with 79 inlets. These long, narrow cannels run inland and are bordered by steep mountains. The longest is Gardner Canal, whose head (the point furthest from the ocean) lies 193 kilometres inland.

Most of B.C.'s coastline is rocky and rugged. There are few sandy beaches. Long Beach is the easily remembered name of the province's longest beach. This 33-kilometre-long beach is part of Pacific Rim National Park on Vancouver Island's west coast.

B.C.'s coastline includes 6500 islands and smaller formations called islets. The largest island on North America's west

Most of B.C.'s coastline is very rugged, like this section of coastline at East Sooke Park near Victoria. (Mark Zuehlke photo)

coast is Vancouver Island. Its shoreline is 3440 kilometres long.

There are two major clusters of islands. Lying between Vancouver Island and the mainland are the 225 Gulf Islands. Off the northern coast of B.C., another 200 islands are known as the Queen Charlotte Islands.

If you just measure B.C.'s mainland coastline from north to south it is 7022 kilometres long. But the true B.C. coastline—including the shores of all the inlets and islands—is really 27 300 kilometres long. That's six times the distance between Vancouver and Halifax, Nova Scotia, on the opposite side of Canada.

Nature's Bulldozer

B.C. was once almost entirely covered by ice thousands of metres deep. During the Ice Age, only the highest mountain peaks in the Rockies and Queen Charlotte Islands were left uncovered.

Acting like a giant bulldozer, the ice dug out deep valleys. Any land that was soft enough for the ice to cut into was gouged away or crushed beneath the ice's massive weight.

For one million years the ice advanced and retreated from the province many times as the earth cooled and heated. Finally the earth warmed to present-day temperatures and the last great ice sheets melted. The melt took 15 000 years. In northern B.C. the ice stopped melting only 7000 years ago.

B.C.'s landscape looks the way it does today because of the bulldozer work done by these ice sheets.

FOSSILS: Clues to an Ancient Past

A long time ago there lived plants and animals that don't exist today. We know about them because we sometimes find their remains, often bones, or imprints of them in stone. These remains and imprints are called fossils.

When people think of fossils they usually think of dinosaurs—the largest animals to ever live on Earth. But there are many other kinds of fossils. In B.C., dinosaur fossils are rare. Only a few dinosaur bones and footprints have so far been found in the Peace River region and near Fernie in the Kootenays.

Over 500 million years ago trilobites dominated the sea. Today, large numbers of their fossils can be found at Walcott Quarry on Mount Field in Yoho National Park. (Frances Backhouse photo)

The largest fossil ever found in B.C. is of an elasmosaur. It was discovered in 1988, on the Puntledge River near the Vancouver Island town of Courtenay. The elasmosaur was a large reptile-like creature with a thin body, a short tail, two pairs of paddle-shaped limbs, a long neck, and a tiny head with long teeth. They measured up to 13 metres (about the length of a school bus) with their head and tail making up half that length. Eighty million years ago, elasmosaurs lived in the ocean and fed on fish.

Since the elasmosaur discovery on the Puntledge River, the fossils of two more of these ancient creatures have been found beside nearby rivers.

In fossil time elasmosaurs are not that old. In eastern B.C. scientists have found the fossil remains of small fish more than 240 million years old. In Top of the World Provincial Park, in the Kootenays, several fossils of long tree-trunk-shaped, spongelike creatures were found in the mid-1990s. They are about 440 million years old.

This elasmosaur skull was found on Puntledge River near Courtenay. Its incredibly sharp teeth helped this creature feed on ancient fish species. (Mark Zuehlke photo)

One of the world's most important fossil sites—the Burgess Shale—is in B.C.'s Yoho National Park. Here, about 140 species of invertebrates (creatures without backbones) have been discovered.

Some of the best plant fossil sites on Earth are found near Princeton, in the Similkameen Valley. Forty million years ago blackberry bushes, as well as gingko, spruce, and apple trees, grew here. But the massive volcanic eruption of a nearby mountain buried them under volcanic ash until fossil hunters found them in the 1980s.

Many fossil sites are protected by law. Removal of fossils from these sites is not allowed. At other sites, such as the beds around Princeton, collection of fossils found on the surface is permitted.

B.C.'s Waterworld

British Columbia is one of the most water-rich areas in the world. Almost one-third of Canada's fresh water—water that, unlike oceans, contains no salt—is found in British Columbia. B.C. has 24 000 rivers and lakes.

Most fresh water is created in one of three ways. It may come from:

- summertime melting of glaciers on the province's highest mountains;
- the melting of winter snows during the spring and summer;
- rain.

If it can, water always runs downhill. This is why rivers run from mountains to the sea. The land that is drained by a river is called a river's drainage area.

The Fraser River has the largest drainage area in B.C. This river crosses the province's entire width and 25 percent of the province's land drains into it. The Fraser

River's headwaters—where the melting of glaciers and winter snows give birth to the river—lie in the Rocky Mountains near Mount Robson. From here the river flows 1368 kilometres to reach the sea south of Vancouver.

The Fraser River grows bigger and bigger during this journey. Smaller rivers running out of nearby hills and mountains flow into the Fraser and add to its size. Some of these rivers, such as the Nechako (Neh-**cha**-ko), Quesnel (Kweh-**nell**), Thompson, and Chilcotin (Chill-**coat**-in) rivers, are almost as wide and deep as the Fraser. Most, however, are quite small.

Other large rivers in B.C. that flow all the way to the Pacific Ocean are the Stikine (Sti-**keen**), Nass, Skeena, and Columbia. The Liard and the Peace are the only major B.C. rivers that do not flow into the Pacific Ocean. They both flow northeast to join the Mackenzie River. The Mackenzie then flows into the Beaufort Sea in the Arctic.

The longest natural lake in B.C. is Babine Lake. Like most of the province's lakes, it is a narrow body of water with steep mountains along its shores. Babine Lake is 177 kilometres long. It is near Burns Lake in central B.C.

Most lakes in B.C. run from north to south. This is because they were formed during the ice age. The ice moving out of the north gouged a trough between mountains. When the ice age ended this trough filled with water from the melting ice. Most of these lakes were once far larger than they are today.

Okanagan Lake originally filled the entire 160 kilometres of the surrounding valley and was much deeper than it is now. Other lakes in this valley, such as Kalamalka, Skaha, and Osoyoos, were once part of this vast lake.

Wild Weather

B.C. experiences some of the most interesting and varied weather in the world. Except for the northeastern corner of the province, B.C.'s weather usually comes from the Pacific Ocean.

Weather travels in air masses—large bodies of air that have the same temperature and water content over their entire surface.

If B.C. were flat, the weather would usually be almost the same everywhere. But B.C. is 75 percent mountains. So, like a roller coaster, air masses have to roll up one side of a mountain and down the other. It's a long ride from the Pacific Coast to the Alberta prairie on the Rockies' eastern side. On the way up one side of a mountain the air cools and rain or snow falls. As it goes down the other side the air warms and dries. As a weather system crosses the province, this process happens at each new mountain range.

B.C.'s mountains are all different heights. Higher mountains are harder for air masses to climb over, so their western slopes will get more rain and snow. If the mountains are low, the weather may be almost the same on both sides.

Victoria has no mountains on either side of it. Weather moves quickly past because it doesn't have to climb any mountains. For a coastal city, Victoria gets very little rain or snow—only 619 millimetres a year. Port Renfrew is just 95 kilometres west of Victoria, but it lies on the western side of the Vancouver Island mountains. So Port Renfrew gets a lot of rain—about 3943 millimetres a year, or more than six times the amount Victoria gets.

Vancouver sits at the western base of very steep mountains of the Coast Mountain range. This is why Vancouver is Canada's wettest city. A little over 150 kilometres northeast of Vancouver is Lillooet. This small town is the hottest and driest community in Canada because it lies on the eastern side of the Coast Mountains.

CATASTROPHIC NATURE

B.C.'s rugged coastline, steep mountains, wild weather, and location in a high earthquake risk zone mean danger as well as beauty. Natural events sometimes threaten human life. Some can also change the landscape permanently.

Avalanches

Snow avalanches are common in B.C.'s mountains. Since 1900 more people in B.C. have died in this type of natural disaster than any other. Almost every winter at least one person is killed after being caught in a snow avalanche.

Most avalanches occur in the Rocky, Columbia, and Coast mountains. When the snow clinging to the side of a mountain becomes too heavy it starts to slide downhill. Like a large wave, the snow hurtles down the mountainside. Anyone in the way will be buried by the avalanche.

Avalanches move fast. In the Rogers Pass avalanches often reach speeds of 180 kilometres an hour (twice as fast as the speed limit on most B.C. freeways).

Most of Canada's avalanches happen in B.C. This is because the province has more steep mountains than other parts of the nation.

The worst avalanche in Canadian history happened at Rogers Pass. On March 4, 1910, 66 men died in this avalanche. Those killed were workers trying to clear snow from the railroad. In the past, most people killed in avalanches were working in dangerous areas.

In recent years people killed in avalanches have usually been enjoying an outdoor sport, such as heli-skiing or snowmobiling. Between 1980 and 1994, 72 people died in avalanches. Only two were not involved in an outdoor sport at the time.

Each winter, avalanches threaten about 1200 kilometres of B.C.'s highways. The provincial highways ministry's Snow Avalanche Section causes the snow to fall before it can reach a dangerous depth. They do this by using explosives, usually fired from large guns. About 1600 avalanches occur near B.C. highways each year. In areas where avalanches often threaten highway and railroad sections, structures called snowsheds are built to cover the route. The sheds are angled so that snow coming down a slope will flow right over the shed and continue down to the slope's bottom.

Landslides

Landslides are common in mountainous country. A landslide occurs when the dirt and rock on a mountain slope break away and tumble to the mountain's base. Most slides are quite small and cause little or no damage.

A few large ones cause lots of damage. One of B.C.'s worst landslides was the Hope Slide. It happened 18 kilometres east of the town of Hope. On January 9, 1965, a 1983-metre-high mountain that was one kilometre wide suddenly began to move. Directly below the mountain ran the Hope-Princeton Highway. Within minutes, 46 million cubic metres of earth, rock, and snow rushed down from the side of the mountain into the

This photo was taken just hours after the Hope Slide buried part of Highway 3 east of Hope and killed four people. (BCARS photo H-04745)

narrow valley below. The slide moved at 160 kilometres per hour. It buried the road under rock and dirt that measured up to 100 metres deep (about the height of a 27-storey highrise building). Four people in cars were killed by the slide.

Earthquakes and Tsunamis (Soo-nom-eez)

B.C. has many earthquakes. About 1000 are recorded here each year. Luckily, in recent history only a few have caused much damage.

An earthquake occurs when the earth's surface moves. Scientists call the point where the movement begins the epicentre. When you drop a rock into a pool of water, ripples spread out in circles from the point where the rock hit. When an earthquake happens, similar ripples spread out from the epicentre across the earth's surface. These ripples are called shock waves.

A pebble tossed into a pool makes only small ripples. A large stone makes bigger ripples. The bigger the rock, the larger the ripples and the more distance they travel. The same thing is true for earthquakes. Small earthquakes happen all the time and we hardly notice them because we are usually far away from the epicentre and the shock waves don't reach us. But a large earthquake sends shock waves far out from its epicentre. These waves can make the ground shake violently and cause serious damage.

Two earthquakes have caused major damage in B.C. On June 23, 1946, an earthquake happened near Mount Washington on Vancouver Island. In nearby towns buildings suffered broken windows, cracked walls, and collapsed chimneys. In Courtenay, a two-storey elementary school was badly damaged when the building's chimneys crashed through the roof into classrooms. Fortunately, it was a Sunday so school was out and the classrooms were empty.

On March 27, 1964, an earthquake with an epicentre 102 kilometres east of Anchorage, Alaska, caused a massive tsunami, or tidal wave. Less than four hours after the earthquake, the tsunami slammed into several communities on Vancouver Island's west coast. Measuring 7 metres high, it was the largest tsunami wave ever recorded in B.C. The villages of Hot Springs Cove and Zeballos (Zeh-**bell**-ose) were hit first and suffered serious wave and flood damage.

Port Alberni was the hardest hit. Houses were thrown up to 300 metres, cars upended and crushed, and boats capsized. Logs moving at more than 32 kilometres per hour were driven into buildings. In all, 58 buildings were destroyed, 320 badly damaged. Total property loss was $10 million. Luckily, nobody was killed or injured. A few hours before the wave struck everyone close to shore had been evacuated. Some escaped just before the wave arrived.

Scientists think B.C. has been lucky. Sooner or later a major earthquake will strike Vancouver Island and the Lower Mainland. But when? Scientists say that between now and the year 2050 there is only a 5 to 10 percent chance of such an earthquake happening.

Volcanoes

Many mountains in B.C. were once volcanoes. Some still are. They are, however, dormant—meaning they are unlikely to erupt any time soon.

The last volcanic eruptions in B.C. ended in about 1750. These eruptions happened at Nisga'a Memorial Lava Bed Provincial Park near Terrace in the province's northwest region.

Scientists think the most likely volcanoes to erupt in B.C. are all located in this part of the province. Hoodoo

Aerial view of a cinder cone
(BCARS photo I-11756)

Mountain on the north side of the Iskut River may be the first to erupt. Standing 1980 metres tall, it has the classic cone shape of active volcanoes. Its crater is now filled with ice and snow. But surrounding valleys are clogged with cooled lava and ash deposits from earlier eruptions.

Not all volcanoes are found on dry land. Off B.C.'s coast three volcanoes stand completely under water. Such volcanoes are known as seamounts.

B.C.'s highest seamount is Union Seamount. It is 3300 metres high. Yet its peak is still 293 metres below the surface of the Pacific Ocean. Union Seamount is 108 kilometres west of Vancouver Island's Estevan Point.

The summits of the other two seamounts are close enough to the ocean surface that scuba divers can swim down to them. Mount Cobb's cone-shaped top forms a giant plate-like platform only 34 metres below the ocean surface. The other seamount is Bowie Seamount. It is nearly as close to the surface as Cobb—just 37 metres.

Forest Fires

Over one-third of all forest fires in Canada occur in B.C. This is because the province is so heavily wooded. Almost 3000 forest fires a year occur in B.C.

More than half of these fires are caused by people. Most of the rest are started by lightning strikes.

The second largest forest fire in North American history broke out on July 5, 1938. It started near the Vancouver Island community of Campbell River. The fire began when sparks from a train engine's smokestack fell on a pile of lumber near the tracks. By the time the fire burned itself out in mid-August, more than 30 000 hectares of forest had been destroyed. The lumber from the trees burned could have built 200 000 homes.

After the fire went out, B.C. decided to plant seedling trees in the burned-out area. They planted about 75 000 seedlings. This was B.C.'s first attempt at reforestation—a practice common today.

The most forest fires in one year happened in 1994. That year more fires were started by lightning than people. From August 3 to August 5, for example, 51 000 lightning strikes were recorded in B.C. These strikes started 1200 fires.

Because B.C. has one of the largest and best forest fire fighting forces in the world, only a small amount of forest is lost each year to fire. Complex computer systems enable firefighters to locate new forest fires within minutes of their starting. By sending out "rapattack" squads, or calling in aircraft known as water bombers, the fires are usually brought under control within a few hours. Rapattack squads are highly trained firefighters who are dropped near fires from helicopters. By getting to a fire while it is still small they can control it quickly and limit the damage caused.

Shipwrecks

The sudden and violent storms of B.C.'s west coast plus its rocky shoreline can be a deadly combination for ships. In all, more than 1100 ships have sunk in B.C. waters—most within the past 100 years. The worst shipwreck in B.C. history was the sinking of the SS *Valencia*.

On Monday, January 22, 1906, the passenger liner *Valencia* struck the rocks of Vancouver Island's west coast near the isolated Pachena Point lighthouse. It was nighttime. A terrible storm battered the ship as it lay on the rocks. Only 37 of the 154 people aboard survived. Until the sinking of the *Titanic* near Newfoundland in 1912, this was the worst shipwreck in world history.

The survivors of the *Valencia* suffered terribly trying to work their way along the rocky coast to the safety of the lighthouse at Pachena Point. Mostly because of this tragedy a life-saving trail was built along this rugged section of Vancouver Island's west coast in 1906.

Now known as the West Coast Trail, it is one of the world's most popular long-distance hiking trails.

Today, most ships that get into trouble off B.C.'s coast don't sink. Each year, more than 250 000 pleasure craft, 6500 fishing vessels, and 3000 merchant ships sail B.C.'s coast. About 2000 of these will send out distress calls. But less than a dozen usually sink. The rest get help from the Canadian coastguard, which patrols these waters.

LIGHTHOUSES

B.C.'s rugged and dangerous coastline is made safer by the presence of 41 lighthouses.

The oldest lighthouse was built at Race Rocks in 1860. Race Rocks is about 16 kilometres west of Victoria. The lighthouse was built from stone blocks brought specially from Scotland to the B.C. coast to build this lighthouse.

The tallest lighthouse on the Pacific coast is at Estevan Point. It stands 38.7 metres tall, about the height of a 12-storey building.

The most westerly lighthouse in Canada is on Langara Island. This lighthouse was built in 1913.

Race Rocks (BCARS photo I-03698)

B.C.'s AMAZING LIVING THINGS

More plants and animals live in the deeply shadowed Sitka spruce rain-forests of Vancouver Island's west coast than in an Amazon jungle. The Okanagan pocket desert near Osoyoos looks empty. But it is home to sage, grass, and birds found nowhere else in Canada. Deep inside caves, where no daylight enters, orchids bloom, spiders spin webs, and crab-like creatures feed in dark, watery pools.

By adding up all the life they find in an area scientists determine what they call its biodiversity. The number and variety of living things found in B.C. give it the greatest biodiversity of any Canadian province or territory. This happens because B.C.'s climate and landscape are so varied. More than 80 000 different types—or species—of animals and plants live here. Some species have large populations. Others are extremely rare or even in danger of disappearing forever.

When we think about the things that live in a place we usually think of the larger animals or plants. Black bears, killer whales, mule deer, moose, eagles, and salmon; pine and maple trees, sage-brush, blueberry bushes, ferns, and wild-flowers. B.C. has all of these animals and plants. But it also has other much smaller and more numerous types of life.

Two young grizzly bears at play (Sean Sharpe photo)

We call animals with no backbone "invertebrates." There are more kinds of invertebrates in B.C. than any other living things. They exist in great numbers everywhere. You'll see invertebrates in tide pools beside the ocean, run across them when you dig in the ground, and have them buzz around your head when you sit in a meadow or outside your home. Invertebrates include flies, worms, bees, sea stars, crabs, and that B.C. coastal favourite, the banana slug. About 70 000 different types or species of invertebrates live here.

Compare that to the number of species of native mammals, birds, reptiles, and fish. In B.C. there are

- 143 mammal
- 454 bird
- 20 amphibian (salamanders and frogs)
- 19 reptile
- 453 fish species

Just 1089 species in total. You could probably count that many invertebrate species in your backyard or local park.

You would also find far more types of fungi growing there than other plants. The fungus family includes such things as mushrooms and the mold that grows on rotting things. In B.C. there are more than 10 000 species of fungi. This compares to 2850 species of trees, grasses, and flowers, which are called vascular plants.

There are more small species in B.C. than large ones. Most are so small you need a microscope to see them.

A Big Word for Forests

Scientists divide the province into regions by looking at the type of forests they find in one place and comparing this to the forest that grows in another place. Each area where a different type of forest grows is called a biogeo-climatic zone. Break this big word down into its three parts—bio, geo, and climatic—and it's easy to remember what it means. Bio is what lives in a zone. Geo is the type of land found there, such as rocky mountains or dry prairie. Climatic is what kind of weather the zone gets. Scientists add these three parts together to determine what kind of trees and other plants will exist there. Once they know what plants live in a zone they know what animal life is there as well. This is because many animals live by eating certain plants. Other animals live by killing and eating these animals or each other.

B.C. has 12 types of forests or biogeo-climatic zones. If you were transported to the middle of one or two forests, you would easily see how different they are from each other. The Coastal Western Hemlock Zone, for example, differs dramatically from the Ponderosa Pine/Bunchgrass Zone.

In the Coastal Western Hemlock Zone the trees are tall and massive. The branches at the top of these trees grow so close together only a little daylight reaches the forest floor. This is the land of the province's great ancient rain-forests. Some of these trees are more than 1000 years old.

In the southern B.C. interior—on the dry valley slopes and ridges of the Okanagan, Thompson, and Similkameen valleys—is the Ponderosa Pine/Bunchgrass Zone. Ponderosa pine trees are often as big and tall as rainforest trees. But they don't grow close together. In fact, they often grow several hundred metres apart. In between the trees grows straw-coloured grass called bunchgrass.

Why is the Coastal Western Hemlock Zone so different from the Ponderosa Pine/Bunchgrass Zone? Mostly because the coast gets a lot more rain than the southern interior. A wet place has more abundant life than a place that is dry. But not all things can live where it's wet. A ponderosa pine would struggle to live there. This tree is specially adapted to live in the dry areas that are its home.

Some other types of trees have adapted to live where it's very high or cold. In B.C.'s northeastern corner there are trees that can survive temperatures of –40° Celsius. They tend to be short with small trunks. Even smaller trees grow just below the highest peaks of the province's many mountains. These alpine trees are so small they look more like bushes than trees. Fierce winds, bitter winter cold, and extremely thin soil cover combine to make it impossible for tall trees to grow here.

Threatened Landscapes

Some of British Columbia's forests that once covered large sections of the province are now far smaller. Logging has reduced the size of some forests to a point where they are in danger of disappearing.

Not only forests are in trouble. Certain kinds of meadows, deserts, grasslands, and even lake bottoms are also endangered. The threat to these areas comes from a variety of causes.

For example, the Garry oak meadows of Vancouver Island and the Gulf Islands are being destroyed by the growth of towns and cities. Many of these meadows have been covered over by roads, houses, and shopping malls. The natural trees, grasses, and wildflowers that live in the meadows are also being overgrown by introduced vegetation, such as Scotch broom. Non-native insects kill more of the natural plants in the meadow areas.

Across the province, more and more lake habitats are being changed forever by a type of underwater plant that is foreign to B.C.'s lake systems. Eurasian watermilfoil first appeared in 1970 in Okanagan Lake. No one knows exactly how it got into the lake. Most people think the weed arrived on the bottom of a boat brought in from outside the province. Some scientists believe it may have been introduced into the lake by somebody dumping the contents of an aquarium tank. However it got into Okanagan Lake, it has since spread throughout the Okanagan Valley's lake system, entered Shuswap Lake, and appeared in lakes throughout the Kootenays, the Lower Mainland, and on Vancouver Island.

Another type of weed, knapweed, entered B.C. from the northern United States. It forces out native grasses in the interior grasslands. Wild animals, such as deer and elk, as well as range cattle cannot get the same food value from eating knapweed as they could eating natural B.C. grasses. Today knapweed covers about 40 000 hectares of B.C. grasslands, but it could spread throughout the entire grassland system.

The following three types of B.C. landscape are most at risk.

Ancient Rainforests

B.C.'s ancient rainforests are part of a forest type that is extremely rare. It never covered more than 0.2 percent of the Earth's surface. Rainforest trees are very old—usually 300 to 800 years. But some trees are more than 1000 years old.

Once rainforests blanketed the coastal shores of the province's mainland and much of Vancouver Island. Only a few areas of this forest still remain because the rest has been logged off. Even more rainforest has been destroyed in other parts of the world. Because of this, B.C.'s rainforest makes up about one-quarter of all the world's remaining rainforest.

In recent years the provincial government has moved to protect some untouched areas of ancient rainforest. Most of the 6700-hectare Carmanah Valley watershed on the west coast of Vancouver Island was made into a provincial park in 1990. Carmanah Pacific Provincial Park was expanded in 1994 to include the upper portion of the valley. Carmanah contains one of the last remaining remnants of the ancient Sitka spruce forests.

The Kitlope Valley, which lies between Kitimat and Bella Coola, is the world's largest untouched ancient coastal rainforest. Many of the trees here are more than 800 years old.

This 317 000-hectare area was protected from logging in 1994. The provincial government is currently working out an agreement on the management of the Kitlope with the First Nations people of this region. When those negotiations are complete, the valley is expected to become another provincial park.

Carmanah rainforest *(Mark Zuehlke photo)*

Garry Oak Meadows

One of the smallest and rarest parts of B.C. is the Garry oak meadow area of southern Vancouver Island and the Gulf Islands. Garry oaks are usually short, twisted, and knobby looking. They grow in meadows of dry grass and wildflowers.

This Garry oak meadow on Christmas Hill is in the very heart of Victoria. (*Mark Zuehlke photo*)

Another unique tree called the arbutus also grows in these meadow areas. It is the only broad-leaf tree in Canada that does not drop its leaves in winter. All other Canadian evergreens are conifers, which are trees with needles. Arbutus also looks unusual because its red bark peels off in paper-thin strips.

When the first Europeans came to where they would eventually build the city of Victoria, Garry oak meadows stretched as far as the eye could see. But as they built farms, towns, and cities the European settlers destroyed most of these meadows.

The few Garry oak and arbutus trees left are usually found only on steep slopes and small hilltops that no one could easily build or farm on. The natural grasses and wildflowers of the meadows have also been crowded out in most areas by people planting other types of grass and bushes.

A rescue attempt is under way to help the Garry oak meadows survive. People on southern Vancouver Island and the Gulf Islands are being asked to plant Garry oak seedlings in their yards. Some people are even turning their yards back into Garry oak meadows by planting the grasses and wildflowers natural to the area.

A Desert in a Pocket

At the very southern end of the Okanagan Valley is the Okanagan pocket desert. It is called a pocket desert because it is surrounded by land that isn't desert. The Garry oak meadows and the Okanagan pocket desert are two of Canada's four most endangered types of country.

The desert is home to sages, prickly pear cactus, and antelope-brush. Once, most of the southern Okanagan was part of this desert. But the building of houses, planting of fruit orchards, and more recent growth of vineyards in the area have destroyed more than 60 percent of it.

Many extremely rare and threatened animals live here. Twenty-two percent of B.C.'s endangered bird, reptile, mammal, or amphibian species call the desert home. More than 250 invertebrate species that are rare or endangered also live in the desert. There are, for example, three types of non-stinging scorpions that live nowhere else in the world. Other species, such as the white-tailed jackrabbit and the pygmy short-horned lizard, have already completely disappeared from this desert.

Unless efforts to save the remaining desert area succeed, the rest of these rare animals and plants may also be lost.

ANIMALS IN THE SPOTLIGHT

There are too many animals in B.C. to describe them all. By looking at a few, however, we can begin to appreciate B.C.'s fascinating animal population.

Zooming Bats

B.C. is Canada's bat capital. There are 16 different bat species here—more than in any other part of the country. Worldwide, though, there are 1065 known bat species. Most live in the tropics. Not many bats like places as cold as Canada.

Like humans, bats are mammals. All mammals are warm-blooded and produce milk for their young.

Bats are the only mammals that fly. They have arms and fingers, just like humans, and these form the framework of their wings. By moving the thumb and fingers separately as they fly, bats are able to do amazing things. They can hover, turn sharply, dive, and climb straight up. Bats are also incredibly fast. Some bats can zoom along at 39 kilometres per hour. To fly this fast a bat beats its wings 10 to 20 times per second.

B.C.'s bats only eat insects. Some catch the insects with their mouths while flying. Others scoop them out of the air with their wings and then slip the bugs up to their mouths by using the wings like spoons.

The Okanagan Valley is the best place in B.C. to see bats. It is home to 14 species.

If you visit the Parliament Buildings in Victoria in autumn or winter you might see one or two of B.C.'s largest bat species—the big brown bat. These bats sometimes fly around inside the building. They whiz about over the heads of the province's politicians.

Roaming Bears

B.C. has two of Canada's three species of bears—black bears and grizzly bears. The province has no polar bears.

You can find black bears almost everywhere. They even wander into Vancouver neighbourhoods and have been seen in downtown Victoria. There are about 120 000 to 160 000 black bears in B.C. Vancouver Island has more black bears than any other part of B.C.—about 10 000.

Male black bears range in weight from 80 to 250 kilograms. Females weigh slightly less than males.

Many black bears aren't black. They are often brown or cinnamon coloured. B.C. also has an unusual black bear that is almost as white as a polar bear. This bear is called a Kermode (Kur-**moe**-dee) bear after the B.C. scientist Dr. Francis Kermode. Dr. Kermode was the first scientist to study this bear. Kermodes live throughout the province, but more are seen in the Terrace area than anywhere else.

There are fewer grizzly bears than black bears in B.C. Still, more grizzlies live in B.C. than in any other Canadian province or territory. Most experts think there are about 13 000 grizzlies here.

It's hard to count grizzlies because they are solitary creatures that don't like to stay in one place too long. A male grizzly often roams over a range of 1000 to 1500 square kilometres. He considers this huge area his home.

A male grizzly can weigh as much as 650 kilograms, but 250 to 500 kilograms is more common. For their size, grizzlies can move very fast—up to 50 kilometres per hour. But they are sprinters, not long-distance runners, so can only keep up this speed for a short time.

These huge animals like to eat delicate, small things. They eat a lot of berries and insects. A favourite food is salmon. They consider salmon brains a special delicacy.

Where can you find the most grizzly bears at once? One place is the Khutzeymateen (**Kootz**-aah-mah-teen) Valley, north of Prince Rupert. The valley covers only 400 square kilometres. From May to October as many as 50 grizzlies crowd into the valley. They come to feed on the berries growing alongside the valley's stream. But the main reason they come to the valley is to eat salmon spawning in the river.

Because of the number of grizzlies here, the B.C. government made the valley a provincial park and Canada's first grizzly bear sanctuary.

Knut Atkinson photo

Deer-Loving Cougars

Cougars are shy and live alone most of their lives. They are found throughout B.C., except on the Queen Charlotte Islands.

Cougars live only in North and South America. Outside B.C. they may be called pumas (**pew**-muz), mountain lions, deer tigers, Indian devils, or Mexican lions.

They are the largest members of the cat family native to B.C. An adult male cougar weighs about 57 kilograms. They have short, usually yellowish-brown, fur.

Cougars love to eat deer. So almost anywhere you find deer you will also find cougars. They also like wild sheep. But they aren't fussy eaters. Cougars will eat anything they can kill. They will eat mice, porcupines, beavers, hares, moose, elk, mountain goats, bear cubs, grouse, coyotes, other cougars, farm animals, and even household pets.

They seldom attack humans, but do find people interesting. Cougars will sometimes spend hours watching people from a rock ledge or the upper branches of a tree. Hikers occasionally discover that a cougar has been following them for many kilometres.

In B.C. there are about 3000 cougars. About 600 live on Vancouver Island. This is because the island has a large deer population.

Dignified Great Blue Heron

With their long necks and slow, careful walk, great blue herons are one of B.C.'s most easily recognized birds. They live throughout southern B.C. and are also found in some central parts of the province. Most great blue herons live on B.C.'s coast or in the Okanagan Valley and south Kootenays.

They eat fish, frogs, and even grasshoppers. Great blue herons hunt by walking through shallow water or standing at the edge in hope that something tasty will pass by. When they spot prey they grab it by striking with their long neck and bill. Because of their hunting habits, great blue herons usually stay close to the shore of the ocean, lakes, sloughs, and marshes. They nest in the trees of woods near favoured hunting locations.

When resting great blue herons hunch their long necks into their shoulders. In flight, their wings move in slow, powerful strokes that allow them to gobble up distance with surprising speed.

The great blue heron is the largest member of the heron family found in North America.

Long-Sleeping Marmots

The rarest mammal in British Columbia, and one of the rarest in North America, is the Vancouver Island marmot. It lives nowhere but on Vancouver Island. Only about 300 are left.

The marmot has chocolate-brown fur, a grey nose, and a bushy tail. It's about the size of a small house cat.

Vancouver Island marmots make their homes in alpine meadows. They group together in small colonies of about eight marmots, including young ones.

Winter lasts a long time in these high altitudes. When the ground is covered with snow they cannot forage for food. So each year the marmots sleep for seven to eight months. They wake up when the snow is gone and the alpine meadow plants they like to eat start growing again. With the beginning of cold

When Vancouver Island marmots want to check what's around them, they sit up on their back legs, as this young marmot is doing. (Knut Atkinson photo)

weather they slip back into their burrows and sleep soundly until spring returns.

Vancouver Island doesn't have a lot of alpine meadows, so there aren't many places for the marmots to settle. Some of these areas have been damaged by the logging of surrounding forests. The marmots have trouble living and reproducing in these areas. Their numbers have slowly been dropping as they find it harder to find suitable homes.

The marmot is one of four vertebrate species (animals that have a backbone) in the province so endangered that it may become extinct within B.C. That would mean not a single member of the species still lived in the province. The other animals in this category are the burrowing owl, the American white pelican, and the sea otter. These other three species live in other parts of the world, so if they become extinct in B.C. they will still exist somewhere. But if the Vancouver Island marmot disappears from B.C., it will be gone from the Earth forever.

Brainy Octopus

Off the shores of B.C. lives the world's biggest octopus—the giant Pacific octopus, also known as the Puget Sound octopus. This octopus can weigh 70 kilograms and stretch 7 metres from the tip of one of its 8 arms to another. Each of its arms is as thick as a large man's upper arm. The more than 200 suckers on each arm are as big as mandarin oranges.

It also has the best developed brain of all invertebrates (creatures lacking backbones). The giant Pacific octopus can learn and remember a lot of things. Researchers think it is as smart as a house cat.

It's a nimble hunter. This octopus can use the tips of its arms to pick up shells and squeeze them open. It then scrapes the meat out from inside the shell with a delicate motion of its arm.

A scuba diver holds a massive Pacific octopus. (RBCM photo)

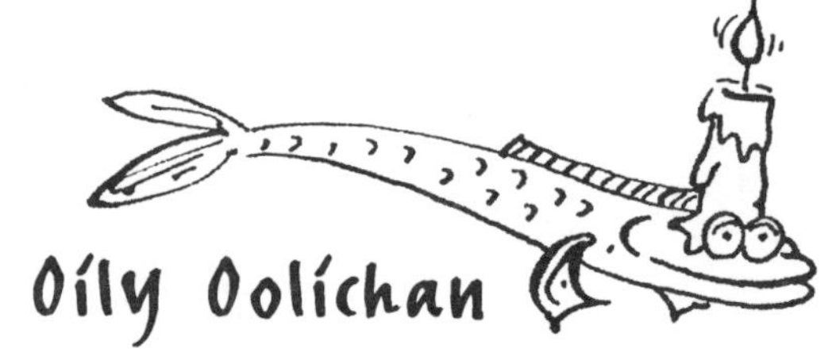

Oily Oolichan

In early spring oolichan (**oo**-lih-kun) swim in from the Pacific Ocean to spawn in many B.C. rivers. Oolichan are also known as eulachon (**yoo**-luh-kon) or candlefish. This small fish is extremely oily inside and out. The oil makes them slippery and hard to hold. When lit, a dead oolichan will burn almost like a candle.

For thousands of years oolichan have been important to the First Nations Nisga'a people in the province's Nass River region. The Nisga'a gather at the Nass River's mouth each spring and capture oolichan with nets. They then boil the fish in large vats for 18 hours, skimming off the rich oil as it rises to the surface of the boiling water.

Oolichan oil doesn't taste fishy. It can be used as it is or made into grease or butter. Traditionally First Nations people used it to flavour food.

Threatened Burrowing Owl

The burrowing owl is named after its home. It lives under the ground in small burrows, as a prairie dog or gopher does.

Burrowing owls are common in many parts of North America. In B.C., however, they live only in the desert and grasslands of the Okanagan Valley and the Thompson region near Kamloops.

Recently B.C.'s burrowing owl population has dropped alarmingly. This is because the owls' home area is being turned into farms and towns. Burrowing owls are now one of B.C.'s most endangered animals.

These birds have a short fat body and long stiltlike legs. Burrowing owls are small compared to most owls—about the size of a robin.

They usually eat small mice and insects. To catch grasshoppers and beetles, burrowing owls often run after insects on their long legs rather than flying.

Burrowing owls don't live in B.C. all year. In the winter, they fly south to warmer places. Each spring fewer of the owls return.

Since the early 1980s scientists have been trying to help increase the numbers of owls living in B.C. They have captured owls in other parts of North America and brought them to the province. They hoped the owls would settle here.

So far the plan hasn't worked very well. No one really knows why, but the owls seldom return in the spring. With continued efforts, burrowing owls may once again be common in the province's desert and grassland areas.

When settlers first came to the Okanagan, they ruthlessly hunted down and killed any rattlesnake they could find. Today, we realize rattlers serve an important role in controlling small mammal populations in dry land areas of B.C. (BCARS photo 66566 D-4216)

Misunderstood Rattlesnake

Most people don't like snakes. Even fewer like poisonous snakes. B.C.'s only poisonous snake is the western rattlesnake. It lives in the southern interior parts of the Okanagan, Kettle, Similkameen, Nicola, and Thompson valleys.

For years many people killed any rattlesnakes they saw. Because of this B.C.'s western rattlesnake is now endangered. Like many animals, rattlesnakes can be dangerous. But they are quite timid and people can easily avoid them.

The western rattlesnake is one of B.C.'s largest snakes. It can be as long as 150 centimetres. A rattlesnake can live 25 years. Throughout its life it keeps growing—so a big rattlesnake will also be an old one.

Rattlesnakes get their name from the horny tip on their tail. When the tail is shaken the tip makes a rattling sound. Rattlesnakes shake their tail as a warning to keep away.

Rattlesnakes stay within one kilometre of their winter den. In autumn they return to the den and hibernate until spring. The dens are deep caverns where 8 to 250 snakes will hibernate at a time.

They eat small mammals, first biting and killing them with venom released from their fangs. The dead animal is then swallowed whole. Rattlesnakes eat mice, shrews, and sometimes squirrels, gophers, and young marmots.

Rattlesnakes pose little threat to humans. In B.C. rattlesnakes bite about three or four people each year. For every 63 people bitten only one will die.

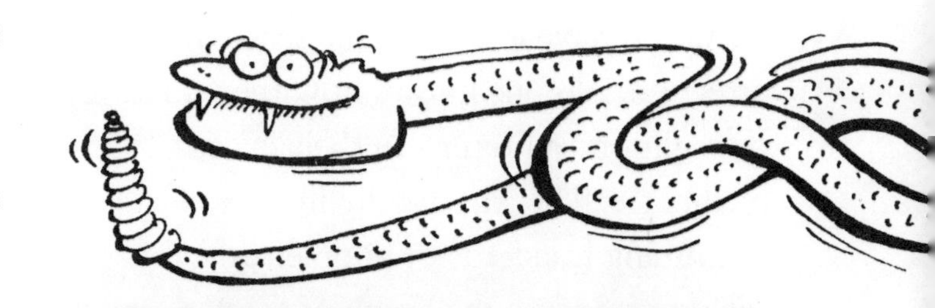

Never-Lost Salmon

Salmon spend most of their lives in the ocean. They only return to the river where they were born to lay their eggs. This process is called spawning. After spawning, Pacific salmon die.

There are five types of salmon in B.C.—sockeye, chum, coho, chinook (the largest), and pink (the smallest).

After completing their 17-day trip from the ocean to the Adams River, these salmon finish laying their eggs on the gravel river bottom. *(RBCM photo)*

Salmon have a remarkable sense of direction. No one knows how they do it, but salmon can return to their exact birthplace. The trip usually involves swimming hundreds of kilometres across the ocean and up the length of many rivers.

The number of salmon spawning in a river each year is called a run. The largest sockeye salmon run in North America takes place at a small river next to Shuswap Lake in the B.C. interior. The Adams River is only 11 kilometres long. Some years millions of salmon come here to spawn.

After being reintroduced to the B.C. coast, the sea otter has made a remarkable comeback. (RBCM photo)

To get to the Adams River the salmon swim 485 kilometres inland. In a 17-day trip they swim up the Fraser, Thompson, and South Thompson rivers, through Little Shuswap Lake and Shuswap Lake, and finally into the Adams River. They do this with no map or compass, yet they don't get lost.

Tool-Using Sea Otters

Until 150 years ago sea otters lived all along the B.C. coast. But Europeans considered their fur valuable and ruthlessly hunted them. They used the fur to make coats, hats, and blankets. In 1929 the last sea otter in British Columbia was killed off the coast of Vancouver Island.

Sea otters, however, survived in other parts of the world. Between 1969 and 1972, 89 sea otters were moved from

Alaska to a few isolated inlets on Vancouver Island's west coast. This small population has since grown to about 900.

The sea otter is B.C.'s smallest mammal that spends most of its life in the ocean. It can stay warm in the cold ocean because of its thick fur coat. To keep its fur in good shape a sea otter spends a lot of time grooming its coat. When it isn't doing this it usually sleeps or eats. Sea otters mainly eat invertebrates, including sea urchins, crabs, and clams.

Sea otters are smart. They are the only mammal other than primates (a group including monkeys and humans) to use tools. Sea otters use rocks to break open shells to get at the meat inside.

They are very social creatures, clustering in large groups of up to a hundred. A group of sea otters is called a raft.

Lazy Sharks

Sharks are one of the oldest creatures on Earth. Modern sharks trace their ancestry back as far as 100 million years. Several types of sharks live in the coastal waters of B.C. Two are especially interesting.

The largest fish in B.C. is the basking shark. It grows to 14 metres in length—about as long as most flagpoles. The basking shark gets its name from its habit of lazily floating or slowly swimming along the surface. Because the basking shark is so huge it moves slowly and

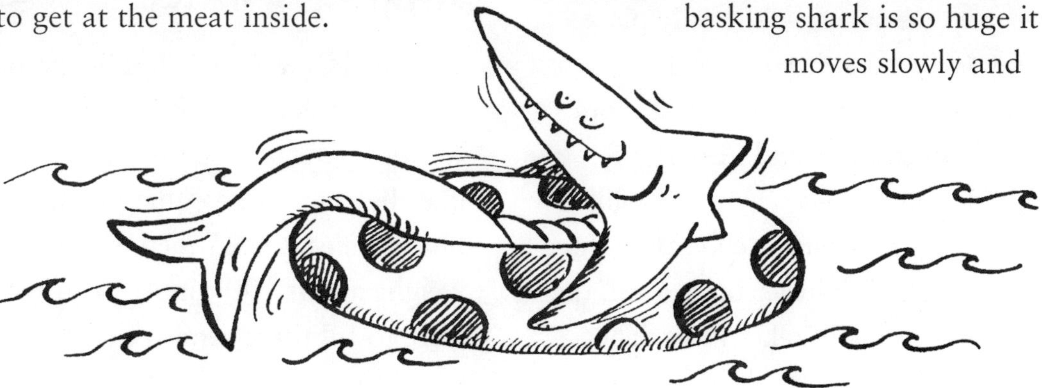

awkwardly through the water. Even stopping or turning takes it a long time.

The basking shark has surprisingly tiny teeth. This is because it feeds only on small animals and plants.

Unlike the basking shark, which lives close to the surface, the mysterious six-gill shark usually stays deep in the sea. This shark averages a length of about 2 metres, but some grow to as much as 5 metres. In many parts of the world the six-gill shark lives as far down as 1500 metres. No daylight reaches that deep and the water is so cold humans would die within minutes.

Yet at several points in the waters around Vancouver Island these sharks do come up to the surface—the only places in the world where they do so. The sharks surface at the south end of Flora Islet, in Saanich Inlet, and in Barkley Sound. No one knows why the six-gill shark chooses to return each year to these shallow waters. Whatever the reason, the warm water seems to relax them. They drift about almost as if asleep.

At Flora Islet, just off the southern tip of B.C.'s Hornby Island, there is a ledge only 15 metres beneath the surface. Here, from June to September, six-gill sharks gather and drift lazily just under the surface. Scuba divers come here from around the world to dive down and mingle with the rarely seen creatures. The sharks even allow the divers to touch them.

Six-gill sharks are not normally dangerous to humans. They usually feed only on small animals, such as crabs and little fish. In September they swim away from Flora Islet, returning to their normal home in the ocean depths.

Singing Whales

The world's largest animal—the blue whale—lives off the B.C. coast. If you were to park two semi-trailer trucks in a line they would be equal in length to a blue whale. It is 25 metres long and weighs about 100 tonnes. You would have to fill three semi-trailer trucks to equal this whale's weight.

Killer whales were once feared by humans, but now we know they pose no threat to people.
(RBCM photo)

The blue whale, like all whales, is a mammal. Yet whales spend their lives in the ocean. They move around by swimming like fish. Once the blue whale was fairly common, but today it is rare and seldom seen.

Blue whales, like most other whales, were hunted almost to extinction by humans. Today hunting of some whale species is strictly controlled and for most species not allowed at all. Only a few countries continue to practise whaling. Despite the decrease in whaling it will be a long time before most whales are common again.

One whale that has returned to its original population size is the Pacific grey whale. There are about 20 000

Killer whales surface in Barkley Sound on Vancouver Island. (RBCM *photo*)

Pacific grey whales. They can grow to as much as 13 metres long. Twice a year the whales swim the length of B.C.'s coastline. From October to December Pacific greys swim from the Bering Sea next to Alaska to Baja California. From February to mid-May they return north.

In the spring, Pacific grey whales swim quite close to the B.C. coast. People standing on the shore of Vancouver Island's west coast can often see them near the shoreline. Other people go out in boats to get a better look.

Another whale often seen on the B.C. coast is the killer whale. Unlike most of the province's other whales, some killer whales spend their entire lives in B.C. waters. About 275 killer whales live in 19 pods (small groups) here. Other killer whale pods and lone whales spend time in the province's coastal areas.

Unlike most other whales, which feed on small fish and microscopic plants and animals called microbes, killer whales eat salmon and other large fish. Some even hunt other mammals who live in the ocean, such as otters, sea lions, and seals.

Humans once feared killer whales, mostly because they had a sharklike appearance and, measuring up to 9 metres in length, looked quite threatening when they came near small boats. Many fishermen used to kill them on sight. But now we know that they are rarely a threat to people.

We also know that whales of all types are highly intelligent. Killer whales are particularly smart. They form close family ties within their pods. They even talk to each other, using various whistling and clicking sounds. Scientists are only just beginning to understand this language.

Another B.C. whale is the humpback, which measures between 10 and 30 metres long. This whale sings songs that last up to 30 minutes. It can repeat the same song over and over again. It's a strange song made up of low moans and sighs that range from high to low notes. Who does the humpback sing for? What does the song mean? No one yet knows.

Nightprowler Wolves

B.C. has one of the largest wolf populations in North America. There are about 8000 wolves here, living in most parts of the province.

You probably won't see a wolf, though. Wolves are very shy of people. They also don't keep human hours. Wolves sleep in the day, travelling or hunting after dark.

Wolves hunt deer, caribou, moose, and smaller animals, such as rabbits and marmots.

Unlike other B.C. carnivores—or meat-eaters—wolves are very social. They live in small packs with parents, pups, and their aunts and uncles. These packs usually number five to eight animals.

A wolf pack will travel over a lot of ground. This ground is considered its territory. Other wolf packs usually stay away from it. A territory can range from 130 to 1500 square kilometres in size.

Wolves are quite common in northern Vancouver Island. This wolf was photographed alongside the Nimpkish River. (Knut Atkinson photo)

MYSTERIOUS CREATURES

They may or may not exist. They are creatures that live in the legends of B.C.'s First Nations peoples. And each year a few people say they've seen these strange animals. The two most famous of these B.C. animals are the ogopogo and the sasquatch.

Ogopogo

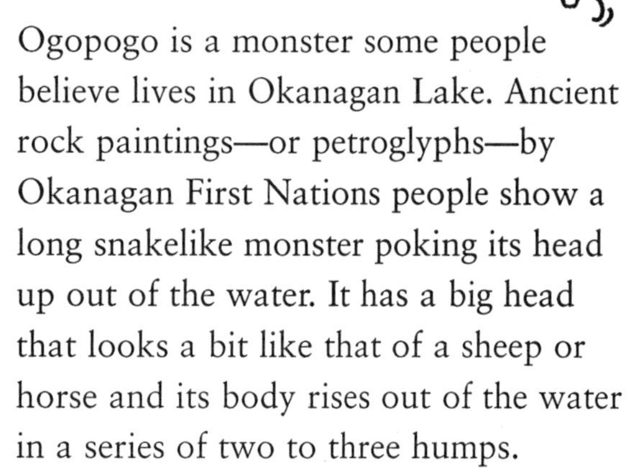

Ogopogo is a monster some people believe lives in Okanagan Lake. Ancient rock paintings—or petroglyphs—by Okanagan First Nations people show a long snakelike monster poking its head up out of the water. It has a big head that looks a bit like that of a sheep or horse and its body rises out of the water in a series of two to three humps.

Ogopogo's home is said to be an underwater cave near Rattlesnake Island on the eastern shore of Okanagan Lake. Rattlesnake Island is directly across the lake from Peachland. Most modern ogopogo sightings happen at night near this island.

The Okanagan isn't the only B.C. lake that might be the home of a lake monster. Osoyoos, Shuswap, Harrison, Moberley, Kootenay, and Cultus lakes are all said to have a creature similar to the ogopogo in them. Although scientists believe that none of these lakes—Okanagan Lake included—could support such a large animal, the sightings continue. There is also a creature called Cadborosaurus that might live in the Saanich Inlet near Victoria.

Ogopogo, however, is the only one of these creatures protected from hunters by law. Whether it exists or not, the ogopogo is a protected species under the provincial wildlife act. It cannot be harmed in any way.

HOW OGOPOGO GOT ITS NAME

Ogopogo is a strange name, even for a creature as mysterious as a lake monster. Where does the name come from?

According to local Okanagan legend, the name Ogopogo was first given to the valley's resident lake monster during a 1926 Rotary club lunch in Vernon. One diner sang an English tune called "I'm Looking for the Ogopogo." The chorus of the tune goes like this:

I'm looking for the Ogopogo, the funny little Ogopogo,
His mother was an earwig, his father was a whale,
I'm going to put a little bit of salt upon his tail,
I want to find the Ogopogo while playing on his old banjo.
The Lord Mayor of London, the Lord Mayor of London,
The Lord Mayor of London, wants to put him in
The Lord Mayor's show!

Ogopogo is what's known as a palindrome. A palindrome is a word that reads—and is said—the same way, whether read from front to back or back to front.

Sasquatch

In the darkest corners of B.C.'s forests creatures called sasquatches may live. Experts who believe in their existence say sasquatches are a type of ape long thought to be extinct, called *Gigantopithecus*. Since 1960, there have been 2000 to 3000 sightings of sasquatches in Canada and the United States.

Sometimes strange footprints are discovered in the forest. They may have been left by sasquatches. These footprints are very big and all the toes are the same size.

By studying the footprints, scientists have decided that a male sasquatch would usually stand about 2.4 metres tall and weigh about 360 kilograms—a good head taller than a very tall human male and four times his weight. Females would be a little shorter, weighing about 225 kilograms.

If sasquatches exist, they probably live in small groups of one male and up to four females and children. They would sleep by day and hunt at night. Their diet would consist mostly of plants, usually berries and roots.

Scientists think there could be no more than about 2000 of these creatures in all of B.C. and America's west coast states.

In other parts of the world sasquatches are called different names. In California they are known as Big Foot. In Asia's Himalaya mountains the creature is called Yeti or the Abominable Snowman.

THE FIRST PEOPLE IN B.C.

B.C.'s First Nations peoples have lived here a long time. Scientists think ancient ancestors of today's First Nations people came to B.C. about 15 000 years ago.

At that time Asia and North America were connected by a narrow bridge of land. This bridge stretched from Siberia in Asia to Alaska. First Nations peoples are believed to have used the bridge to come from Asia to North America.

About 6000 to 8000 years ago people stopped crossing from Asia into North America. Eventually the ocean covered the bridge. It was no longer possible to walk between the two continents.

When First Nations people tell their history they usually say they have always lived in B.C. Some First Nations creation stories tell of how First Nations people were created here by gods or spirits. A Haida (**Hie**-dah) creation story, for example, tells of how they were released into their home on the Queen Charlotte Islands from the inside of a clam shell.

To understand just how long First Nations people have been in B.C., think of this. The longest any non-First Nations person's family could have lived in B.C. is about 5 generations. A First Nations person, however, can easily be part of a family that has lived here for 200 or more generations.

The First Nations people of British Columbia are not all the same. Before Europeans arrived here the First Nations people divided the province into several independent countries, just as the United States and Canada are different countries today. The Haida, for example, lived in the Queen Charlotte Islands and the Ktunaxa (Too-**nah**-hah) lived in the Kootenays. The people in each of these nations spoke a language and had customs that differed from those of people in other parts of B.C.

First Nations peoples mixed with their neighbours. They traded food and goods, often worked together for a common cause, and sometimes fought wars with each other.

Most of the First Nations peoples' languages, customs, religion, and types of art have survived to this day.

Redressing a Wrong

When Europeans first came to B.C. most felt that the First Nations peoples who lived here did not own the land. Because First Nations peoples lived differently than they did, practised different religions and customs, and were not white in colour the Europeans thought they were less human. They used this belief to justify their taking the land away from the First Nations peoples without paying for it.

Usually the Europeans took the land without getting any kind of agreement—or treaty—from the First Nations people. Between 1851 and 1858, only 14 treaties were signed between First Nations peoples on Vancouver Island and the Europeans settling there. No other treaties would be entered into until 1900 when five First Nations' bands in the Peace River region signed what is known as Treaty Eight.

During these years, however, the First Nations peoples of B.C. were often forced to move to small areas of land called reservations. Once they were resettled the rest of their traditional lands were opened to Europeans for development.

Beginning in 1912, the First Nations peoples of B.C. started trying to get the provincial and Canadian governments to recognize that their lands had been wrongfully taken away. It took 78 years of struggle on their part to finally get this fact recognized.

In 1990, both the provincial and Canadian governments started negotiating treaties with B.C.'s First Nations peoples. The treaties determine what compensation will be paid the First Nations peoples for lands they have lost and establish a framework to give them self-government over their lands and people.

These land claims negotiations—as they are usually called—will take many years to resolve.

First Nations Art

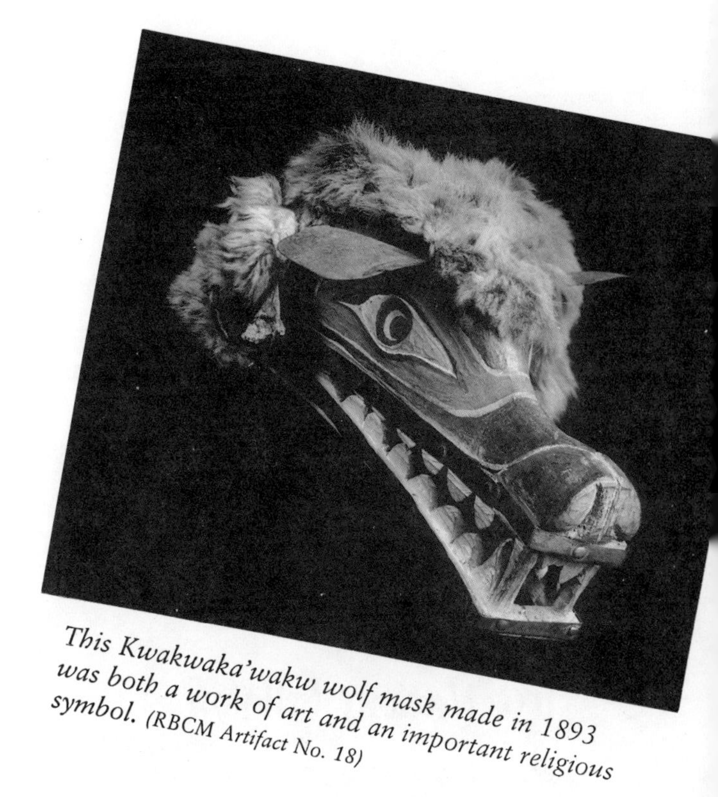

This Kwakwaka'wakw wolf mask made in 1893 was both a work of art and an important religious symbol. (RBCM Artifact No. 18)

B.C.'s First Nations peoples have always worked with wood, reeds, paints, and metals to create art. They weave images on baskets; carve pieces of wood into boxes, masks, and totem poles; paint pictures on stones; and make jewellery from pieces of silver and copper. Usually First Nations artists portray the animals they see around them. They also like to show the spiritual world that exists alongside the everyday world. This spiritual world gives each animal a unique character and special powers. In their art they try to show both what the animal looks like and what kind of spirit it has.

First Nations artists often work on things that are part of everyday life. They weave pictures into the sides of baskets used to carry food and water. Or they carve beautiful masks that are used for religious ceremonies or in plays.

First Nations Religion

Before Europeans came to North America most First Nations peoples shared a common form of religion. They believed that everything in the world—trees, mountains, animals, rivers—had a spirit. If you treated a river or animal's spirit with respect it would respond kindly to you. But if you failed to show respect the spirit might cause you harm.

They also believed that every person had a spirit which looked out for their well-being. This spirit was called a guardian spirit. Young people discovered their guardian spirit during a puberty trial. At puberty, by fasting or carrying out some difficult task, First Nations youths would have their spirit revealed to them during a dream or trance. If during that dream, for example, a young person saw a wolf it might mean he had the spirit of a hunter. It also would mean that wolves would try to protect that person in times of trouble.

When Europeans settled here they tried to force First Nations people to give up their traditional religion. Many First Nations children were taken from their families and sent to live at schools run by churches. Here, they were forced to adopt Christianity. Some First Nations religious and social customs, such as the potlatch, were made illegal.

But the First Nations religion was never completely lost. Today, many First Nations people are again practising their traditional religion.

Potlatches

The potlatch was one of the most important B.C. First Nations ceremonies. A First Nations family or chief would mark a major event by hosting a potlatch.

As part of the ceremony, the person holding the potlatch would usually give many gifts—blankets, carved cedar boxes, canoes, food, fish, and other items of personal value—to the guests. People would be invited from far away to these large ceremonies.

A potlatch might take years to plan. They often lasted for days. During a potlatch there would be spirit dancing, religious feasts, theatre performances, and the giving of gifts.

People did not hold many potlatches. A powerful chief might host only four during his entire life. Most people would never hold one.

Europeans who settled in B.C. did not understand potlatches. They found the ceremonies frightening. They also thought it wrong to give away so many gifts.

In 1884, missionaries working in the First Nations communities demanded that potlatches be declared against the law. This was done.

From then on anyone holding a potlatch was punished. In 1922, for example, Kwakwaka'wakw (Kwalk-**walk**-ee-walk) chief Dan Cranmer held a potlatch at Alert Bay. Some experts say it was the largest potlatch ever held. A few days after it started, however, the police came. They ordered the people who had come from all over the west coast to go home. They also forced everyone to give up Cranmer's gifts to them. Chief Cranmer refused to stop the potlatch and was put in jail. Because he stood up for their way of life, he became a hero to the First Nations people.

In 1951, the law against holding potlatches was cancelled. Now First Nations people can hold potlatches without fear of being punished.

Totem Poles

Like potlatches, totem poles also play an important role in the life of First Nations people of the B.C. coast. Carved out of the trunks of trees, totem poles serve many purposes. Today, they are also one of the most important types of art produced on the B.C. coast.

Some totem poles tell the story of a family. Others tell a legend of a spirit. Common animals that are carved on totem poles are beavers, bears, wolves, sharks, ravens, whales, eagles, frogs, and mosquitoes.

Most totem poles are carved out of red cedar trees. Before Europeans came to B.C. the poles were painted black, red, and blue, or sometimes white and yellow. The paint was made by mixing minerals and vegetable matter.

Poles came in many heights. They could range from one metre to fifteen metres tall.

Totem poles were often put up during potlatch ceremonies. So when potlatches were made illegal the art of making totem poles was almost lost. But when potlatches were again allowed, the art form also thrived.

Today, many totem poles are carved each year and sold to cities and art collectors around the world. Several communities in B.C. have large numbers of totem poles. The poles at Alert Bay, Kispiox, and Skidegate are among the best in the province. Alert Bay used to be home to the world's tallest totem pole. It stood 53 metres tall. But in 1994, as part of the 15th Commonwealth Games celebrations, Victoria put up a 55-metre-high totem pole. This is now the world's tallest.

Haida clan poles at Skidegate in Queen Charlotte Islands (BCARS photo I-15825)

Nuu-chah-nulth petroglyphs at Sproat Lake on Vancouver Island
(RBCM photo PN 11733)

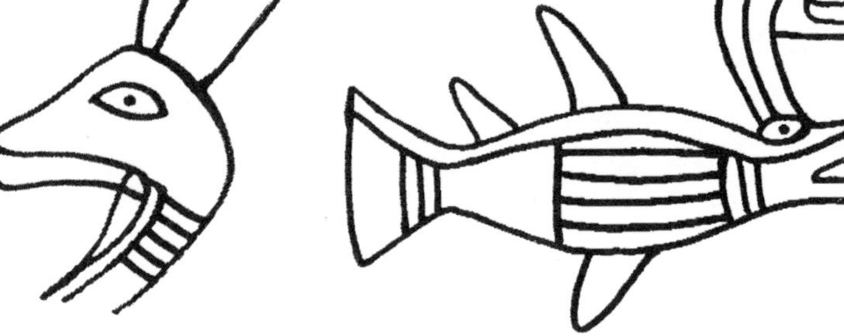

Pictographs and Petroglyphs

A long time ago the ancestors of First Nations peoples used rock faces to tell of their lives and their spirit world. They either painted images on the rocks or carved them into the rock with sharp tools. The painted images are called pictographs. Carved images are called petroglyphs.

There are many pictograph and petroglyph sites in B.C. Petroglyphs are more common on the coast and pictographs in the B.C. interior. On the B.C. coast there are more than 500 petroglyph sites.

Usually the images are of humans, animals, or geometric designs.

The two most easily visited petroglyph sites are both on Vancouver Island. They are Petroglyph Provincial Park south of Nanaimo and Sproat Lake Provincial Park, near Port Alberni.

Petroglyph Provincial Park has stone carvings that are about 10 000 years old. The images are of humans, birds, wolves, lizards, and sea monsters.

Pictographs can be found at Marble Canyon Provincial Park near Lillooet, in Wells Gray Provincial Park, near the hot springs at Kootenay National Park, and at Big Rock in Tweedsmuir Provincial Park.

A TIME OF CHANGE

Barely 200 years have passed since the first non-First Nations person came to British Columbia, but few of the people who were living then would recognize the province as it is today. Recent B.C. history is amazing, for so much has happened in such a small period of time.

Captain James Cook lands at Nootka Sound in 1778. He is the first European to set foot on what will become B.C. But the Nuu-chah-nulth people who live in the sound and warmly welcome him have been here for thousands of years. (BCARS photo PDP00494)

European Explorations

Spanish explorer Juan Perez Hernandez was the first European to see British Columbia. Hernandez sailed up the coastline in 1774. He didn't manage to land because a storm blew his ship away from shore. He did, however, claim the coast as part of the Spanish Empire.

Captain James Cook arrived four years later. He landed at Nootka Sound on Vancouver Island's west coast. Cook was greeted by the Nuu-chah-nulth (New-**chah**-noolth) people living in the sound. They shouted something to him, but Cook only heard the word "Nootka." He decided they were telling him who they were. They were actually giving him instructions for entering their harbour. Because of this misunderstanding Europeans called the Nuu-chah-nulth people Nootka for more than 200 years.

Ignoring Perez's earlier claim, Cook said all of British Columbia was now part of the British Empire. Neither explorer bothered to ask the First Nations people living here whether they wanted to join any empire.

Spain and Britain quarrelled over which country owned this area for 14 years. In 1792, Spain gave up its claim. B.C. became part of the British Empire.

A year later, explorer and North West Company fur trader Alexander Mackenzie entered British Columbia from the east by travelling up the Peace River. First Nations people guided Mackenzie and nine companions overland from the Peace River to the Pacific Coast. On July 21, 1793, Mackenzie first saw the Pacific Ocean at the head of Dean Channel, near Bella Coola. Mackenzie was the first European to travel across North America from one ocean coast to the other.

B.C.'s first European settlement was built in 1794. It was near today's Fort St. John. The community was a fur-trading outpost.

Europeans initially explored the interior of British Columbia by following its great rivers. In 1808, Simon Fraser and 23 others journeyed down the Fraser River. They followed the river from what is today Prince George to its mouth at the Pacific Ocean.

The trip took 35 terrible days. "We had to pass where no human being should venture," Fraser later wrote. The worst part of their trip came at a narrow, rocky gorge (or canyon) south of today's Boston Bar. Inside the gorge were river rapids running at speeds of 47 kilometres an hour. The rapids were too rough for Fraser and his companions to go through in their canoes. They had to leave them behind. Luckily, they were able to find some First Nations people who agreed to guide them through the gorge. The First Nations people of this area had built a system of trails—including wooden scaffolds hung from the cliff faces—through this section of the canyon. Following the guides, Fraser and his companions were able to pass safely through this dangerous place. Fraser described the gorge as being like the "gates of hell." It is now known as Hell's Gate.

The dense forests, steep mountains, and narrow valleys of B.C.'s mainland slowed the coming of European settlers.

For many years the only Europeans interested in British Columbia were fur traders.

In 1843, the Hudson's Bay Company built Fort Victoria on the southern tip of Vancouver Island. Six years later the first settlers came from Britain to set up farms near the fort. In 1851, Vancouver Island was made a British colony.

These gold panners working alongside the Fraser River were but a few of the more than 30 000 prospectors who came to B.C. for the province's first major gold rush. (BCARS photo A-01958)

Gold Rush Fever

In early 1858 gold was discovered in the Yale region of the Fraser River. News of this strike soon reached the rest of the world. In just three months, between May and July, 30 000 hopeful miners poured into the B.C. mainland. These miners included about 7000 Chinese immigrants, the beginning of the province's large Chinese community. At the same time, African American settlers came to Victoria and set up various businesses.

New communities sprang up alongside the lower Fraser River. Fort Langley, until then a small fur trading outpost,

The thriving main street of Barkerville during the Cariboo gold rush (BCARS photo A-03786)

grew rapidly as stores were opened to sell goods to the miners heading upstream.

The mainland's first colonial government was formed here the same year. A year later, however, the government shifted to New Westminster—a community created by the gold rush.

Soon the Fraser River gold strike was over. But the miners didn't leave B.C. Instead they headed farther inland seeking new gold fields. Miners panned almost every river in south and central B.C. in their search for gold. In 1860, the biggest of all B.C. gold rushes started in the Cariboo region.

On August 21, 1862, William Barker found gold on Williams Creek in the Cariboo. Within a year the town of

Barkerville had sprung up in the middle of the Cariboo forest. It quickly grew to a population of 10 000, with stores, hotels, and dance halls.

Many of the miners became rich. Barker dug $600 000 worth of gold from his claim. But like most of the miners he spent his earnings very quickly. He was soon a poor man again.

For several years Barkerville was one of the largest cities in North America. But the gold fields around it were quickly emptied. Most of the people left. By 1871 it was a ghost town—a place of empty buildings slowly falling apart. In 1958, however, Barkerville was restored and turned into a provincial park. Today, thousands of people visit this remote community each year to get a taste of what gold fever felt like.

The gold rush at Barkerville was the last of the great B.C. gold rushes. Most of the miners left the province. A few stayed, however. So did some of the store owners and business people who had built communities to provide services and goods for the miners.

The Cariboo gold rush led to the building of a road into the province's interior. Called the Cariboo Road, it ran for 650 kilometres from Yale to Barkerville. When it was completed in 1864, the road opened up the interior for settlement.

Joining Canada

In 1867 the eastern part of Britain's North American colonies formed together to become Canada. This act was known as Confederation. The B.C. mainland had only become the colony of British Columbia in 1858. Vancouver Island was a separate colony. The two colonies were united in 1866. Two years later Victoria became the new colony's capital.

These Chinese workers were among the many who risked their lives to push the Canadian Pacific Railroad through the dangerous Fraser Canyon section of the cross-Canada line. (Vancouver Public Library 66958)

It was not until 1871 that B.C. voted to become part of Canada. To encourage B.C. to join, the Canadian government promised to build a railroad from the Atlantic to the Pacific Ocean. Such a railroad would allow Canadians to move easily and cheaply from one side of the country to the other.

Building the railroad was hard for such a young country. It took 15 years. Crews worked from both sides of the country, laying track towards each other. Because there were so many mountains to cross in B.C., that section of railroad took the longest to lay and cost the most money.

About 15 000 of the people working on the B.C. section of the railroad were Chinese immigrants brought here for this purpose. At least 1500 of these workers died in accidents. When the work was finished the B.C. government forced some of the Chinese to return to China because European settlers thought there were too many Chinese settling in B.C.

On November 7, 1885, the "last spike" was finally driven at Craigellachie, near Revelstoke. The country was now connected from sea to sea.

The railroad reached the Pacific Ocean at the small community of Vancouver. As a result Vancouver quickly grew into a major port city. By 1901 it was the largest city in B.C. with a population of about 27 000. Victoria had a population of 24 000. Few European settlers lived anywhere else in the province.

By 1901 the communities of Vancouver and Victoria already included people from every corner of the earth. In 1877, the first Japanese settlers had arrived. Soon about 10 000 Japanese had settled in B.C. Sikhs (Seeks) and Hindus also

Sikh (right) and Japanese (left) immigrants arrive in Vancouver harbour at the turn of the century. The Sikh immigrants on this ship were mainly ex-soldiers of the British Army.
(Vancouver Public Library photo 3027)

arrived during this period from the British colony of India. All of these people, however, were treated unfairly by the European settlers who outnumbered them.

Growing Pains

Between 1901 and today the province's population grew rapidly. Most people worked in farming, forestry, fishing, or mining. Many settled near the railroad in areas where there was good farm land. The Lower Mainland, the Okanagan Valley, and the east coast of Vancouver Island became home to most of the province's population. Today, more than three-quarters of B.C.'s population lives in these three regions, which contain barely one-quarter of the province's total land area.

During the Great Depression many single men were put in relief camps such as this.
(Vancouver Public Library photo 8834)

In 1914 British Columbians joined the rest of Canada in fighting in World War I. More than 60 000 Canadians died during the four-year war.

The war changed the nation and B.C. During the war many women worked in offices and industries because most of the men were away fighting. When the war ended the number of women working outside the home continued to increase.

After the terrible experience of the war Canadians hoped for a better future. They wanted a good job and world peace. For a while both hopes looked possible. Then, in 1929, the Great Depression began. The Great Depression put millions of people out of work around the world. In Canada—and British Columbia—almost one-third of Canadians could not find jobs.

Many men travelled across the country searching for work. Women and children often had to move in with any relative who would give them a home. Throughout B.C. the government opened relief camps where jobless men had to live in order to get food, shelter, and 20 cents a day in wages. Most of these men were then put to work building roads by hand.

The Great Depression ended in Canada when World War II began in 1939. Businesses and farms that had been closed all through the depression reopened to provide food and equipment needed to fight the war. More than one million Canadians served in the war against Germany, Japan, and Italy. About 42 000 died.

In B.C., the war was used as an excuse to take away the property of the province's 20 000 Japanese Canadians. The Japanese Canadians were also forced to move from their homes on B.C.'s coast to camps in the province's interior. These camps were very similar to prisons. The government sold the property of Japanese Canadians and kept the money. After the war ended in 1945 their property

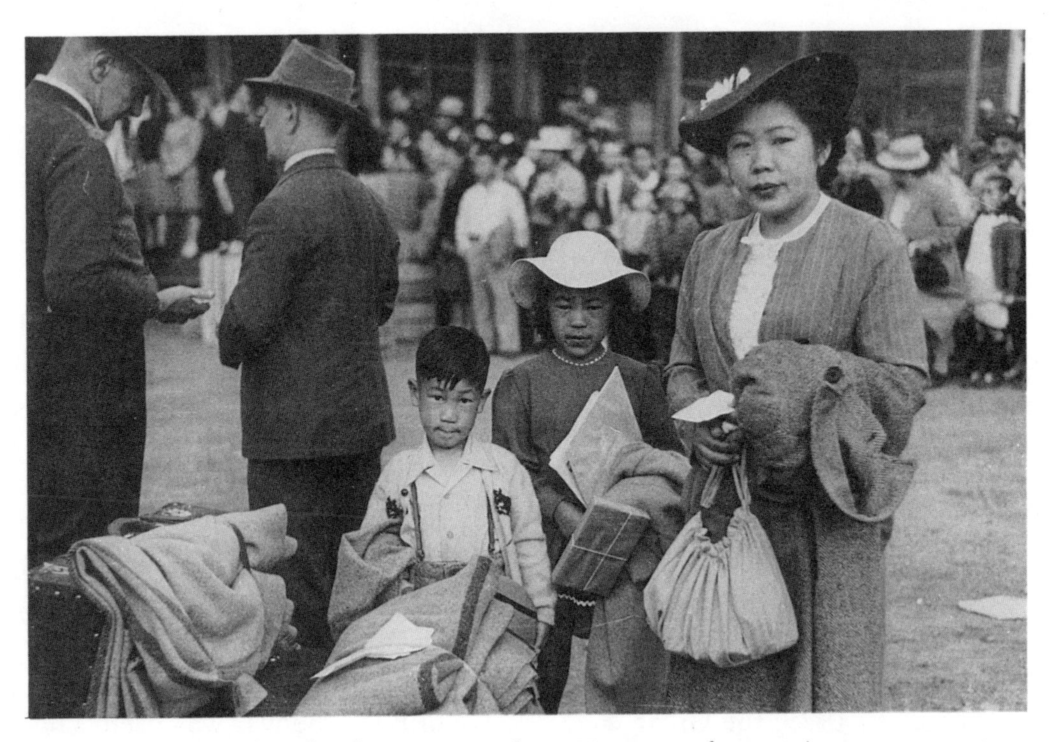

A Japanese Canadian family prepares to leave Vancouver for an internment camp in the B.C. interior. The father, like most Japanese Canadian male adults, had been interned several months earlier. The families were not always sent to the same camp as the fathers. (National Archives of Canada photo C57253)

was not returned. Many of the Japanese Canadians were also forced to decide whether to move to eastern Canada or be sent to Japan—even though most had never been to Japan or even outside B.C. before the war. Known as the Japanese Canadian relocation, this event is one of B.C. history's darkest moments. In 1988, the Canadian government apologized for the relocation and paid $300 million to the survivors and their families as compensation for the wrong.

Modern Times

After World War II the economy of B.C. grew rapidly. Aiding this growth was the construction of highways across the province, which linked most B.C. communities more closely together than had been previously possible in such a large, mountainous country. Today, there are about 22 000 kilometres of paved highways in the province and 21 000 kilometres of unpaved highway. These highways cross some 2700 bridges.

In areas where there are no roads or the roads are very poor, there are few communities. Despite the province's large highway system most of B.C. can only be reached by water, air, or hiking trail.

The land that makes joining communities so difficult continues to drive the economy of B.C.—forestry, mining, fishing, and agriculture.

Construction of good roads, however, has helped tourism become important in recent years as more of the province can be easily reached. Every year about 24 million people—or about eight times the province's population—come to B.C. as tourists. Most tourists visiting B.C. come from other Canadian provinces or from the United States. Of the American tourists about 1 in 6 comes from California.

Tourists from other parts of the world come mainly from Japan, the United Kingdom, and Germany. Each year the number of tourists from these three countries increases.

Many people in B.C. also make a living by working in businesses that provide things other people need. These are called service industries.

The province has also attracted artists, writers, film makers, musicians, and actors. This has led to the growth of a strong cultural industry. About 43 000 people work in B.C.'s cultural industries—about half as many as work in the forest industry and nearly double the number working in B.C.'s fishing industry.

B.C.'s film industry is particularly strong. Vancouver is now the third largest film-making centre in North America.

In the future, more people will work in B.C.'s service, tourism, and cultural sectors—or in the small, but growing, high-technology and science industries—than in the traditional areas of forestry, fishing, agriculture, and mining.

A fishing boat operates in the rich fishery of Dixon Entrance in the Queen Charlotte Islands. (BCARS photo I-15467)

A KALEIDOSCOPE OF PEOPLE

Most of the 3.5 million people in B.C. trace their family roots back to Europe. About 40 percent of British Columbians have a British heritage. Another 30 percent come from other European groups—including 8 percent who are of German origin.

B.C.'s largest non-European ethnic group is Chinese. About 9 percent of the province's population is Chinese. The other two major ethnic groups in B.C. are East Indians (4.4 percent) and First Nations peoples (3.7 percent).

Just as British Columbians come from many places around the world, they also hold a wide range of religious beliefs.

Most British Columbians are Christians. There are about 603 000 Roman Catholic, 420 000 United Church, and 328 500 Anglican Church followers in B.C. These are the largest of the Christian churches in the province.

Spiritual leader Paul Verigan and Doukhobor followers gather at Brilliant, B.C. in 1924. *(BCARS photo 47562)*

After Christianity, Sikhism is the second most practised religion with 74 550 followers. This is followed by Buddhism, which has about 36 500 believers, and

Jehovah's Witness with about 33 650. There are about 24 900 Muslims in B.C., 18 000 Hindus, 16 000 Jews, 5000 Unitarians, and 3500 Baha'is.

One of B.C.'s oldest Christian faiths is declining. In 1961, there were more than 10 000 Doukhobors (**Duke**-uh-borz) in B.C. Today, there are only 3700 practising Doukhobors.

The Doukhobors—a Russian Christian group—came to Canada at the turn of the century to escape persecution in their home country. They were pacifists and vegetarians, and did not drink alcohol or smoke tobacco. Because of their pacifist beliefs they refused to serve in the Russian army. The Russian government denied their citizenship and put many of them in detention camps.

In 1910, about 6000 of the Doukhobors who had come to Canada moved to B.C. They settled throughout the Kootenays, especially in the Castlegar region. Most of the province's Doukhobor community still lives in the Kootenays.

The Doukhobors wanted to live together in one area. For B.C.'s Chinese community, on the other hand, the decision to live in Chinatowns was mostly forced on them by the province's European residents.

With the start of the gold rushes in 1858 Chinese immigrants began arriving in B.C. European settlers encouraged Chinese immigrants to come to B.C., but forced them to work for lower wages than they would pay a fellow European. They also hired Chinese immigrants to do types of work they didn't want to do.

The European settlers also wanted to make sure that they always greatly outnumbered the Chinese and other Asian peoples. To make certain this was the case they made all Asian immigrants—including Chinese—pay to come into the country. This was called a head tax. The tax was so expensive that it was impossible for most Chinese to bring their families with them. Instead young men came alone. As a result many lived without families all their lives. Others only stayed in B.C. for a short time. After a few years they returned to China to start families.

Because European settlers treated the Chinese immigrants badly, the Chinese tended to live together in one section of a city. Both Victoria and Vancouver developed such areas, which became known as Chinatowns. The gold mining town of Barkerville had Canada's first Chinatown.

Until the 1930s, Vancouver had laws that stopped Chinese settlers from buying property outside of Chinatown. This further encouraged the Chinese in Vancouver to settle in just one area.

Today, both Victoria and Vancouver still have Chinatowns. They are, however, more shopping districts than places where most Chinese live. In both cities the large Chinese populations live throughout the community.

For a long time most new British Columbians came to the province from other countries. Since the 1960s, however, most people moving to B.C. have come from other Canadian provinces. In 1992, for example, about 41 000 people moved to B.C. from other parts of Canada. During the same year only 29 000 came from other countries.

Fan Tan Alley in Victoria's Chinatown was once home to several opium dens. Today, it houses small specialty shops and is known as the narrowest commercial street in North America. (BCARS photo I-03386)

Recently more people have come to B.C. than have moved away from the province. This means the population of B.C. is growing ever larger.

SUPERLATIVE B.C.

Canada's tallest tree. The hottest Canadian city. The nation's wettest place. Its highest city. Listed alphabetically, here are some of the records that make B.C. Canada's superlative province.

Agriculture

Farming has always been important in B.C. This is surprising as very little of the province can be farmed. Most of B.C. is too mountainous or high to have the rich soil needed for farming. Only 17.5 percent of the province's land can be used for agriculture.

There are about 19 000 farms in B.C. Almost half of these are in the Fraser Valley. The Okanagan grows almost all of B.C.'s fruit. About 85 percent of B.C.'s grain is grown in the Peace River region.

The province's dairy cows produce about 510 million litres of milk per year. That's enough to allow each person in B.C. to drink half a litre of milk a day.

Each year, B.C.'s chickens lay nearly 720 million eggs. So many berries are grown in B.C. that each person could eat about 18 kilograms a year and there would still be berries left over. Ninety-five percent of all cranberries grown in B.C. are sold to one customer—Ocean Spray—which provides packaged cranberries, cranberry sauce, and cranberry juice to most of North America's food stores.

The most profitable crop in B.C. is ginseng (jin-seng). It is grown for its root. Many people think the ginseng root can make people healthier. It is ground up and made into a powdered tea, pills, and other supplements. A hectare of harvested ginseng sells for about $300 000. By comparison, a hectare of tomatoes sells for about $10 000. Most ginseng is grown in the Thompson and Okanagan valleys.

Ainsworth Hot Springs

Located near Kootenay Lake, these hot springs have the highest mineral content of any in Canada. They are also the only hot springs in B.C. heated by molten rock boiling up from the earth's core.

Babine Lake

B.C.'s longest natural lake is Babine Lake. It is 177 kilometres long. The lake is 36 kilometres north of Burns Lake in the province's northwest.

B.C. Ferries

B.C.'s ferry fleet is one of the world's largest. The ships move vehicles and passengers back and forth among the coastal islands and the mainland.

Each year more than 21 million passengers and more than one million vehicles will ride the ferries.

Birds

The rhinocerous auklet (rye-**noss**-er-us **awk**-let), tufted puffin, Anna's hummingbird, yellow-billed cuckoo, and the pigmy nuthatch are just a few of the fascinatingly named birds found in B.C. The province's native bird species number 454. Another 51 have been introduced, giving a total of 505.

More bird species (297) breed in B.C. than in any other Canadian province. Some breed almost nowhere else on Earth. Between 60 and 90 percent of all Barrow's goldeneyes breed only in B.C., as do 20 to 35 percent of all bald eagles, and 74 percent of ancient murrelets.

B.C. lies on a major bird migration path—the Pacific flyway. Many bird species travel the length of the province during their twice-a-year migrations. For example, the world's entire population of western sandpipers lands at various southern B.C. mudflats twice a year. They stay a few days to rest and feed before flying on.

When people move into an area, they often fill in marshlands and estuaries to create farms and towns. This destroys the lands that birds need for feeding, resting, and breeding grounds. This is one of the main reasons that more than 80 of B.C.'s bird species are in danger of extinction within the province.

Scientists have now discovered the importance of marshes, estuaries, swamps, and bogs to birds and other wildlife. New areas are being protected as bird sanctuaries. More than 240 bird species visit the 344-hectare Reifel Bird Sanctuary in Delta each year. The 7000-hectare Creston Valley Wildlife Management Area just west of Creston is frequented by 250 species.

Carmanah Giant

This ancient Sitka spruce, towering 95 metres above the rainforest floor, is Canada's tallest tree. Carmanah Giant is taller than most 30-storey buildings. It stands in the middle of a grove of other massive trees in Carmanah Pacific Provincial Park on Vancouver Island's west coast. The trail leading to the tree is closed to the public to protect the area. Nearby Heaven Tree, however, can be seen. Heaven Tree is 81 metres tall.

Chemainus

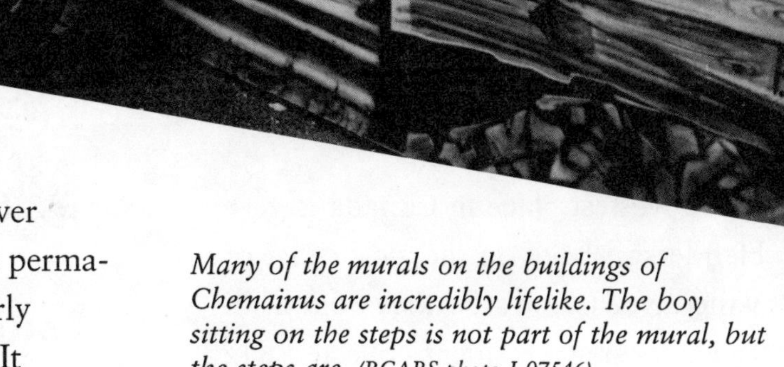

Many of the murals on the buildings of Chemainus are incredibly lifelike. The boy sitting on the steps is not part of the mural, but the steps are. (BCARS photo I-07546)

This small community on Vancouver Island is home to Canada's largest permanent outdoor art gallery. In the early 1980s the town's sawmill closed. It looked as if Chemainus might become a ghost town—but the people decided not to leave. Instead they changed their mill town into a major tourist attraction. Artists were hired to paint murals that showed the region's history on downtown walls. Every year about 250 000 people visit Chemainus to see the murals. Because of this plucky little community's refusal to die, Chemainus is known across Canada as "The Little Town That Did."

Climate

Some parts of B.C.'s west coast get up to 220 frost-free days a year—more than anywhere else in Canada. All of B.C.'s coastline is ice-free every day of the year.

The warmest place in Canada on a day-to-day basis is Sumas Channel, 60 kilometres east of Vancouver. Sumas Channel enjoys an annual temperature of 10.7° Celsius.

On April 19, 1986, it started raining in Victoria. The rain fell non-stop for 33 days. This is the longest wet spell ever to hit a major Canadian city.

The wettest place in Canada is Henderson Lake on the west coast of Vancouver Island's Barkley Sound. In 1931, its single resident collected 8122.5 millimetres of precipitation. He fled the place in 1936. It has remained uninhabited ever since.

Canada's least sunny community is Stewart. The sun shines here an average of only 949 hours per year.

B.C. holds all Canadian snowfall records. Greatest average annual: 1433 centimetres at Glacier. Most in one season: 2447 centimetres at Mount Copeland, near Revelstoke. Most in one day: 118.1 centimetres at Lakelse Lake, near Terrace, on January 17, 1974.

Douglas Lake Cattle Ranch

This is Canada's largest cattle ranch. It was established in 1884. The ranchers here run about 19 000 cattle on 200 000 hectares of grazing land. Douglas Lake Cattle Ranch is located near Merritt in the heart of the Interior Plateau grassland country.

Fairweather Mountain

B.C.'s highest mountain is Fairweather Mountain. It stands 4663 metres high. Fairweather Mountain is located in the province's extreme northwest corner. Its western and southern slopes lie in Alaska. Mount Waddington, with an elevation of 4016 metres, is the tallest mountain lying entirely within the province.

Not too far away from Fairweather Mountain, in the Yukon Territory, stands Canada's highest summit—5950-metre-high Mount Logan.

Grand Forks

From 1898 to 1919 this small community on the western edge of the West Kootenays was home to the largest copper smelter in the British Empire and the second largest in the world. The Granby Smelter processed copper, gold, and silver.

Greenwood

Today fewer than 1000 people live in this small community. But in 1897, a nearby gold rush led people to think it would become one of the biggest places in western Canada. So they declared the West Kootenay community a city. The gold ran out and the people left. But Greenwood retains its past glory by being known as Canada's smallest city.

Kimberley

Look up, look way up, and you'll see Kimberley. Situated in the Rocky Mountains west of Cranbrook (itself the sunniest city in the province), Kimberley is Canada's highest city. It stands 1113 metres above sea level. Kimberley is also home to the world's largest working cuckoo clock.

Mica Dam

Mica Dam is the highest earth-filled dam in North America and the eleventh highest in the world. It rises 242 metres above the Columbia riverbed. The dam opened in 1973. It is located about 150 kilometres north of Revelstoke at the end of Highway 23.

Mica Dam is just one of many in B.C. that provide hydro-electric power. Almost all of B.C.'s electrical power is produced when the powerful flow of rivers passes through specially built dams. More than 70 percent of all the province's power comes from dams built on just two rivers—Columbia and Peace.

The electricity created in B.C. is sent throughout the province over 69 000 kilometres of power lines.

Mount Macdonald Tunnel

It's 14.6 kilometres long and cuts right through the heart of two mountains—Mount Macdonald and Cheops Mountain. This amazing tunnel is North America's longest railway tunnel.

Building the tunnel took four years. It was completed on the twelfth day of the twelfth month at twelve noon in 1988.

To build the tunnel two crews dug toward each other. It would have been easy for the crews to have missed each other deep inside the core of the two mountains. To ensure this didn't happen, laser and satellite technology tracked the two crews and guided them in a straight line to a meeting place in the centre.

Nanaimo Bars

Were the tasty sweet Nanaimo bars invented in Nanaimo, B.C.? No one really knows. But the small city has an official recipe for the bar. Here it is.

The Ultimate Nanaimo Bar Recipe

Bottom Layer

1/2 c. (120 mL) unsalted butter
(European-style cultured)
1/4 c. (60 mL) sugar
5 Tbsp. (75 mL) cocoa
1 egg, beaten
1 3/4 c. (435 mL) graham wafer crumbs
1 c. (240 mL) coconut
1/2 c. (120 mL) finely chopped almonds

Melt first three ingredients in top of double boiler. Add egg and stir to cook and thicken. Remove from heat. Stir in crumbs, coconut, and almonds. Press firmly into an ungreased 8-inch (20-centimetre) square pan.

Second Layer

1/2 c. (125 mL) unsalted butter
2 Tbsp. plus 2 tsp. (40 mL) cream
2 Tbsp. (30 mL) vanilla custard powder
2 c. (500 mL) icing sugar

Cream butter, cream, custard powder, and icing sugar together well. Beat until light. Spread over bottom layer.

Third Layer

4 squares of semi-sweet chocolate
(1 oz. [28 g] each)
2 Tbsp. (30 mL) unsalted butter

Melt chocolate and butter over low heat. Cool. When cool, but still liquid, pour over second layer and chill in refrigerator.

New Hazelton

In 1914, this small community 67 kilometres north of Smithers was caught up in the largest gunfight in western Canadian history.

The year before, seven outlaws had gotten away with the armed robbery of a railway train in New Hazelton. The success of that robbery led the same gang to return. Again they held up a train.

This time, however, the townspeople realized what was happening and ambushed the robbers as they rode out of town. A short, furious gunbattle raged. More than 200 bullets were fired. When the smoke cleared, three outlaws lay dead and three were wounded. One had managed to escape. He had the money.

Okanagan Lake Floating Bridge

The Okanagan Lake Floating Bridge was North America's first floating bridge. It is 640 metres long.

Crossing Okanagan Lake at one of the lake's narrowest points, the bridge is the valley's only link between eastern and western shores. The bridge took two years to build. It was finished in 1958.

Powell River

The world's second shortest river is Powell River. It's near the B.C. community that shares its name. Powell River is only 500 metres long, running from Powell Lake into the ocean.

Quesnel Lake

The deepest fjord lake in the world is Quesnel Lake. A fjord lake is created by glaciers scouring a valley bottom during an ice age. Most B.C. lakes are fjord lakes.

Quesnel Lake is 530 metres deep. Although that is deep, it is much shallower than the world's deepest lake. Lake Baikal, in eastern Siberia, is an amazing 1619 metres deep. It is also the largest lake in the world.

Ripple Rock

This rock sank more ships than any other hazard on the B.C. coast. Up until 1958, 20 large ships and over 100 smaller vessels went down after striking it. More than 100 people died when these vessels sank.

Situated just north of Campbell River, in the Seymour Narrows section of the Strait of Georgia, Ripple Rock was cursed by sailors.

Finally the Canadian government decided to get rid of the rock by blowing it up. It took 30 months to build a tunnel from a nearby island to a point deep beneath Ripple Rock.

Engineers bored two holes upward from this shaft into the rock's core. These holes were then stuffed with explosives.

At 9:33 a.m. on April 5, 1958, Ripple Rock—long a hazard to Strait of Georgia shipping—was destroyed in the largest non-nuclear peacetime explosion in history. (BCARS photo D-08490)

At 9:33 a.m. on April 5, 1958, Ripple Rock was blown up. It was the largest non-nuclear peacetime explosion in world history. The entire top of the rock shattered into many pieces. Only remnants of the rock, lying deep below the surface, remain.

Ships now sail without fear through Seymour Narrows.

Rocky Mountain Trench

Running 1400 kilometres from the province's border with the United States to just south of the Yukon Territory, the Rocky Mountain Trench is North America's longest valley. It lies entirely within B.C.

The trench is incredibly narrow. It never exceeds 20 kilometres in width. Sometimes it narrows to 3 kilometres. On either side it is flanked by steep mountain ranges.

The Columbia River flows down most of its length.

Water

B.C. is one of the most water-rich areas in the world. It contains almost one-third of Canada's fresh water. All this water flows through 24 000 lakes, rivers, and streams that cover almost 2 percent of the province's total land area.

Waterfalls

British Columbia has the four highest waterfalls in Canada: Takakkaw (503 metres), Della (440 metres), Twin (274 metres), and Hunlen (253 metres). Takakkaw is nearly ten times the height of Niagara Falls. Yoho National Park is home to both Takakkaw and Twin.

B.C. has thousands of other waterfalls. Anywhere in the province there are usually waterfalls close by.

Index

Photographs are shown in **bold**.

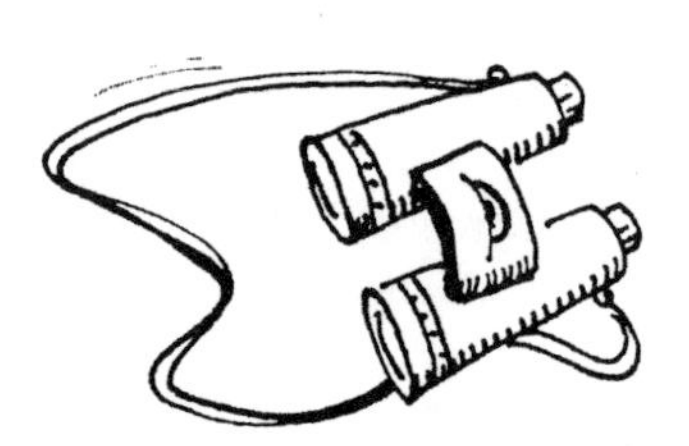

About the Author

Rosemary Neering

Mark Zuehlke is a full-time writer who lives in Victoria. His other books include *The B.C. Fact Book: Everything You Ever Wanted To Know About British Columbia*, for which this book can be considered a companion volume. He has also published *Scoundrels, Dreamers & Second Sons: British Remittance Men in the Canadian West*; *The Vancouver Island South Explorer: The Outdoor Guide;* and is co-author of *Magazine Writing from the Boonies*. His magazine articles have appeared in such publications as *The Financial Post Magazine, Equinox, Canadian Business*, and *Canada & The World.*

Mark draws the topics he writes about from the things he loves, including history; outdoor activities, such as hiking, sea kayaking, and cycling; and travel.